HUMAN HARVEST

by

George Graham

with Illustrations by
Patrick Stacy

authorHOUSE®

AuthorHouse™
1663 Liberty Drive, Suite 200
Bloomington, IN 47403
www.authorhouse.com
Phone: 1-800-839-8640

First published by AuthorHouse 3/19/2009

ISBN: 978-1-4259-9883-7 (sc)

Printed in the United States of America
Bloomington, Indiana

This book is printed on acid-free paper.

One

The bitter cold was unimportant. It had started to numb his joints about an hour ago. That was when he had first stepped into this filthy, decrepit alley to hide. And though his cramping lungs screamed out in protest to the frigid air they were inhaling, he did not move from his strategic position. Silently, he continued to watch the entrance to the city morgue across the street.

About a week ago, weather forecasters had predicted that the arctic cold front, which had been traveling mercilessly south through Canada, would soon reach and then stall here in Washington. It was not unusual for the nation's capital to have its share of cold weather in January. But since this cold front had arrived two days earlier, the temperature hadn't gotten above the freezing point. That was very unusual. Washington was poorly equipped to handle this cold spell. Utilities were having trouble maintaining power due to the intense demand for electricity to power heaters to the MAX throughout the city. That was why the streetlights were all without power, so that every possible kilowatt could be diverted to household usage.

That made the alley surrounding this mysterious figure completely pitch black. *That was good*, he thought to himself. It was vital that he not be discovered. The body he sought within that morgue held the answers to questions of monumental importance. Questions which must be answered tonight.

Finally, the two patrol officers for whom he'd been waiting exited the morgue to continue their overnight shift of the Southeast. He could hear the crunch of the frozen snow under their tires until it eventually faded into the distance.

As he crossed the street, an observer might have wondered why he left behind no footprints in the snow or why he exhaled no frosted breath. But there were no observers. The homeless and the drug addicts that normally infested these streets had been rounded up at the start of this cold spell to prevent them from freezing to death. Even the most desperate of prostitutes dared not venture outside at night to brave this intense arctic air.

The 3:00AM morgue staff consisted of four members: a coroner, his assistant, a security guard, and a janitor. On a normal night, any or all of them might be on the main floor. But this was no ordinary night.

The figure from the alley reached the locked main entrance door. He reached his fingers into the crevice between the door and the doorframe. With a rending of metal he tore out the deadbolt barring his path. He slid the door open and entered. The silence was eerily overpowering.

As he had expected, the main desk, which should normally have been staffed by a guard, was empty. Eight black&white monitors behind the desk were fed by stationary security cameras. Six of the eight showed no activity. One monitor depicted the janitor going about his floor buffing duties. It was monitor #8 that broadcast the location of the other three staff members. They stood in the main autopsy room staring at the body that had been brought in to them. Even on the small monitor, their facial expressions of fear and confusion were apparent.

Washington, D.C. had averaged nearly one homicide per day for many years now. Most of those bodies passed through this morgue. Bodies dead from gun-shots, stabbings, beatings, poisonings, drug overdoses, mutilations, strangulations, hit & runs, and even explosions had all lain on this table at one time or another. But never a body like this.

It was to this autopsy room that the figure went.

Coroner Terrence "Terry" Loman was no coward. While serving as a field medic for two tours in The Vietnam War he had become numb to fear. The mayhem and carnage that he'd seen almost daily back then on the battlefield forced his young mind to withdraw from everything but the task at hand.

"Don't become close to your fellow soldiers, they may die tomorrow. Don't think about the wives or children of the enemy soldiers, you may not be able to kill them tomorrow." It was advice he'd learned and lived by.

He became so mentally isolated, that he was unable to practice medicine when he returned from Vietnam in '73. His mind was unable to retrain itself to be warm and caring or even interested in patients. So he instead practiced medicine for dead patients. Forensics.

But as he stood here with his assistant and the curious front desk guard, he was quite afraid. He had never seen a body like this. What kind of mind could think to do this to another human being? And why??

All of them jumped as the door from the hallway swung suddenly inward. The man that entered the room was of less than average height. He was slim but muscular. A black hood covered his head. The rest of his body was clothed in black outerwear and boots. But it was his eyes that they would remember forever.

Those eyes glowed with an intensity that none of the three men had ever seen before. They could almost feel him stare into their souls. When he spoke, it was with an unholy accent that none of them had ever heard before.

"I do not wish to harm you," he said. **" I will examine that body briefly, then I shall depart."**

"No! You'll turn around and put your hands on that wall!" responded the guard. His voice quivered with fear just a bit because this stranger emanated an aura of power. And though the stranger was much smaller than the guard, he made no attempt to comply with the guard's command. Even as the guard crossed the room with his baton drawn, the stranger made no movement.

"One more chance!" shouted the guard with false bravado. "Turn around and grab that wall with your hands, or your face is gonna grab my club!"

Still the stranger did not move. As the guard raised his baton, the stranger darted out his hand faster than any cobra could strike. He grabbed the guard's forearm and squeezed. The baton fell immediately to the floor, but the stranger squeezed harder.

Terry Loman knew that the cracking he was hearing was from the fracturing of the ulna and radius bones of the guard's forearm. The noises that followed were sickeningly new to Loman because he had never heard those bones being pulverized into powder by the force of a man's grip. Out of the corner of his eye, Terry saw his assistant charge the fighting men. But the guard had passed out from the pain and was thrown aside by the stranger. A roundhouse kick landed flush on the assistant's nose. A mini-explosion of blood burst out as the assistant's nasal cartilage splattered flat onto the left side of what was once a handsome face. The assistant passed immediately into unconsciousness.

"Enough delay! Tell me of your findings," demanded the stranger.

Loman cooperated immediately. "This subject is d-dead f-from blood loss." Loman suddenly realized that he was stuttering uncontrollably from terror. "B-But he's lost *all* of his b-blood. There isn't s-so much as a drop in any vein, artery or organ. All other b-body fluids are intact but th-there is no b-blood whatsoever." Loman continued, "There was n-not even a drop at the c-crime scene. This man's blood has been removed with skill beyond that of even the finest surgeon. It's impossible. But true."

Loman had been staring at the body as he spoke. The thought occurred to him that it almost looked like a vegetable that had been squeezed of all its juice. Only the dry pulp and seeds remained under the skin. He shuddered as he again tried to think of what sinister mind could think of a method to do this. The stranger was standing over the body, closely examining the neck of the corpse.

Soon, without a word, the stranger turned to leave. The guard was whimpering in the corner where he had landed in the earlier fight. The assistant coroner still lay unconscious in the doorway. The stranger began to step over him to leave, but then saw and smelled the blood oozing from the assistant's splattered nose. He knelt down beside the assistant.

So much blood.

So close.

Red.

Thick.

The stranger tried to pull away, but could not.

The blood.

Warm.

Smooth.

He dipped his finger into the assistant's moist nasal cavity. He brought the finger up to his mouth.

In that moment he would decide to give in to this sweet temptation or to wipe his finger clean and walk out.

With an iron will, the stranger forced himself to wipe the blood off his finger, onto the unconscious assistant's shirt. He turned, took the police scanner radio from the guard's belt clip, walked out, and disappeared into the night.

Two

Merlena Bennett was wondering what in the world she was doing here. She'd been wondering that a lot lately. This wasn't the America that she'd dreamed about her entire life while growing up in her native country of Jamaica. As a little girl, she'd been told stories of an America that had gleaming cities of big, bright, beautiful buildings. A place where the people were friendly and caring. Most importantly, America was supposed to be the land of opportunity, where hard work would be rewarded with lots of money. When "Lena's" visa finally came through two years ago, she immediately left for Washington, D.C. - the very capital of this wonderful country.

But this wasn't at all what Lena had expected. She soon learned that her educational achievements in Jamaica were considered worthless over here. She had extensive accounting experience for a major hotel in Negril, on Jamaica's northern coast. But to be an accountant here, she learned that she needed to become "Certified". To become certified she would need to go to school. To go to school she would need money. To get money she would need a good job. A good job for her would be accounting. But to be an accountant, she needed money for school. AAHHH!!! It was such a never-ending circle of frustration! How could any immigrant hope to get ahead in this country?

So instead of school, she had only been able to get a job as a cashier at the local hardware store. The pay wasn't good, but it was the best job she'd been able to find in her two years here. At least it paid the rent. But the rent was for an old, cramped apartment in a run-down building here in the projects of Southeast Washington.

Her job and her apartment weren't the only things making Lena miserable. Last winter was the first time that she had ever experienced weather below sixty degrees Fahrenheit. At the time, she had actually been looking forward to experiencing the ice and snow. As she stepped out one morning after last year's first snowfall, she wiped out on the unexpectedly slippery ice and nearly sustained a concussion. That had been enough winter in the U.S.A. for her.

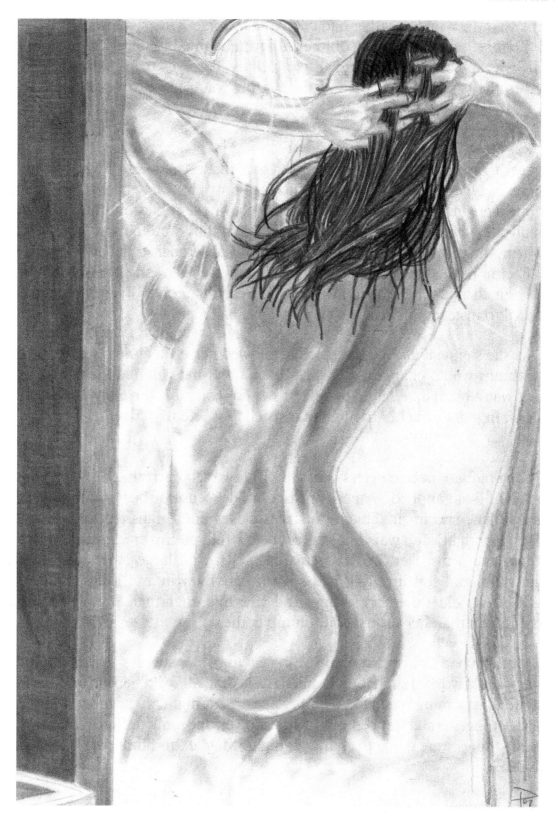

This year the winter weather had been much worse. The past few days had featured the most severe cold she could ever have imagined in her wildest thoughts. The air was so cold that she had to try to keep her eyes nearly shut when she walked to the bus stop or she felt as though the water in her eyes would start to freeze.

It was now 7:00AM and she was preparing to make that frigid walk to the bus to get to work for her 8:00AM shift. Once again she asked herself why she was here. Maybe her sisters, all six of them, got it right. They had all found men and gotten pregnant at an early age. Now most of them had multiple kids. And although they lived a simple lifestyle in Jamaica, they were happy. The weather was warm, the people were friendly, and life moved serenely at its own Caribbean pace. The more Lena thought about it, the more homesick she became. If things didn't soon change for the better, Lena would use the money she'd started saving for school to instead purchase a one way ticket back home.

As she stepped into the shower, she allowed herself a glimmer of hope that maybe things would change. After all, she had her first date in almost a year tonight. It was a blind date set up by one of her co-workers. Normally she wouldn't chance a blind date, but her friend had insisted that "Kenny" would be perfect for her.

Lena had not been dateless because of her looks. In truth, she was a beautiful girl. Not in an anorexic-American-supermodel sense of beauty. Rather, Lena was an athletic specimen. Thick, muscular calves and thighs led to firm round buttocks. Her tight, slim waistline was set below full, plump breasts and muscular shoulders and arms. Her face was equally pretty with large dark eyes, a small straight nose, and soft lips. She had smooth, ebony skin and long hair in box-braids. She was older than her siblings and of a different father. Her physique was much different than her sisters' soft, plump bodies.

Merlena had always put men secondary to career success. Since coming to America, she'd worked such long hours that she had allowed herself no time for a social life. But coming home to an empty apartment night after night was becoming maddening. As she stepped out of the shower, she smiled. She definitely had a feeling - things were going to change tonight. Maybe this blind date wasn't such a bad idea.

As for now, off to work.

"You ready for tonight girl?" Lena's friend Tanya shouted to her from her cash register stand. "You are gonna love my cousin Kenny. He's handsome, a great dresser, and a real gentleman. He ain't been able to find the right woman but you're perfect for him."

"And you're sure he's right for me?" asked Lena.

"Listen to Tanya, honey. You gonna be a different woman after tonight. Girl, you might actually smile."

"Don't forget Lena, I'm here if things don't work out." This latest person to join the conversation was Leon. He was twelve years old. He worked on weekends bagging purchases; not coincidentally he was usually bagging at Lena's register. He'd had a crush on her since the day she'd walked in the store to fill out a job application.

"I told you before Leon, I'm all yours the day you turn twenty-one," Lena said, then playfully blew him a kiss. Leon caught it in mid-air and rubbed it on his cheek.

Lena was giddy the rest of her shift. The right man in her life could make her very happy indeed. She could hardly wait to finish up and get home. She didn't know where Kenny was taking her tonight, but Tanya had hinted that she should dress fancy. At 6:00PM Lena clocked out, hurried home as best she could through the awful, frozen streets, and prepared for her blind date.

He arrived and rang her doorbell at 9:00PM, an hour late. Lena's hopes of finding a mate ended as soon as she opened the door. Kenny was dressed in a bright red suit with unbelievably gaudy matching bright red shoes. His hair was braided in nappy cornrows, and when he smiled, he revealed two gold front teeth. His hair, his breath, his clothes, even his skin reeked of the smell of cigarettes and possibly marijuana. He apparently had no problems with her appearance. He stopped leering at her breasts only long enough to crane his neck around to try to get a peek at her ample booty. When he introduced himself, he did so with the most unromantic line she had ever heard. "Hey sexy, I'm Kenny. What's your name again?"

Lena didn't know whether to introduce herself or slam the door in his face. Slamming the door was very tempting, but she was already dressed to go out, and it had been so long since she'd experienced some nightlife. She reluctantly decided to let him in. She knew that this date would lead to absolutely nothing, but at least she got to spend a night out.

Kenny announced that he was going to take her to a hot club. Normally, Lena would have thought this to be a foolish choice for a blind date. The pounding music would drown out any conversation of two people trying to get to know each other. But Lena wasn't trying to get to know Kenny, she wanted a night out. Afterward she planned to shake his hand, thank him for the date, and say good-bye.

Kenny, for his part, didn't care about conversation either. He just wanted to find a way to get this full-bodied woman out of her dress as soon as possible.

Driving to the club seemed to take an eternity. The inside of his car smelled like a veritable cigarette factory. At least three times she had to pry his hand off of her thigh as he talked endlessly about his plans to produce a rap album when he secured his finances. Finally, they arrived at the club.

The arctic air and lightly falling snow outside had dwindled the usual Saturday night crowd down by about fifty percent. Despite the small crowd, the club was jumping. The deep hip-hop bass was powerful enough to make Lena's chest vibrate. Multicolored lights flashed in rhythm to the music. Somewhere a fog machine layed a light mist throughout the club. Lena hadn't danced since she left Jamaica and she made up for it this night. She wasn't dancing so much with Kenny (who was making repeated trips to the bar) as much as she was dancing to the rhythm and beat that was stirring her soul. She joined some other single young ladies and let loose. Almost two years of pent up frustration was being released on the dance floor as her athletic, shapely body writhed and undulated to the pulse of the pumping music. More than a few men got slaps from their dates when they turned to gaze at the sheer sexuality of this fine Caribbean woman's dance.

Kenny, however, was becoming a problem. He had become out-of-control drunk. Lena was having real trouble keeping his aggressive, pawing hands off of her body. Finally she could take no more and yelled as best she could above the music to Kenny to take her home. Kenny, in his drunken stupor, misunderstood this as a signal to take her home to bed. As soon as they exited the club into the freezing night air of the parking lot, Kenny slid his hand onto Lena's rump.

"Enough!!" Lena shouted. She had lost all patience for this rude, crude, smelly man with his bright red shoes.

"C'mon girl, I got a big back seat, let's get to the car so you can gimme some," responded Kenny.

"You're not gettin' anything Kenny! Back off, don't make me hurt you!" This was no idle threat from Lena. She had alot of toughness and strength to go along with her muscular body. She'd also always had a strange, innate affinity for fighting. Actually, throughout her entire life, Merlena had excelled in any sort of intense competition. No one else in her family shared this natural gift. It wasn't something that she had ever been able to understand or explain. Somehow, something inside of her just seemed to click on and take her over when she was confronted. Whether it was a situation as healthy as an athletic challenge, or as dangerous as the rape attempt that she was about to face, her opponents had always gone away severely defeated.

But Kenny could not have known, and would not have cared, about Merlena's physical gifts. He continued to advance. "I spent alot of money on you tonight woman; you need to be givin' me some."

"Gwon Boy! Lef Meh!" Merlena's full island patois came out to order him away as her anger intensified.

Suddenly, Kenny grabbed Lena by her long braids and attempted to pull her head down to his groin.

Lena gave Kenny a devastating right-handed body blow to the abdomen, just below the ribs. Then another. Another. Her left fist then smashed into his right ear so hard that she ruptured his eardrum. A left uppercut under the chin was followed by a crushing right fist flush against his mouth. Kenny was overwhelmed by her fury. He could barely keep his balance because of the inner-ear injury and was choking on blood from his bleeding mouth. But Lena wasn't done. One more powerful right punch to the head knocked Kenny to the ground. Lena then unloaded on him a savage kick to the groin. Then another. Then one more.

Lena began to walk away from Kenny's blubbering form. There were no witnesses to their scuffle. It was far too early for any other patrons to have left the club. The cold kept windows tightly shut of anyone living nearby that may otherwise have heard Kenny's screams.

The cold.

Somehow, during the fight, Lena had forgotten the cold. She could now feel the frigid air numbing her unprotected legs below her coat and dress. Her feet sent icy messages of frozen pain from her high-heel shoes. Obviously, she didn't have a ride home with Kenny. She remembered seeing a mini-mart a few blocks away on the ride here. She would call a cab from there.

Kenny began to get up from his spot about twenty feet behind her. "Bitch!!" he shouted. "Damn Psycho Bitch!! Ho! Get back here. I'll show you what a ho's good for! Damn dyke!!" His shouting began to fade as she continued away from him. Kenny continued to shout even though she was out of his sight. "Bitch!"

"Bitch!"
"Bitch!"
"Dyke!"
AAAAARRGHHAAAHAAGGG..............

What the hell was that scream? Lena asked herself. *Was it some trick Kenny was trying? No one could fake a scream like that. Did someone just mug him?* Lena had been in that parking lot just seconds ago. No one else was nearby at the time.

Against her better judgment, Lena turned back toward the parking lot.

Kenny was gone. Lena looked between, and even under, the rows of cars, but he was nowhere to be found. She retraced her footsteps in the snow to the site of their fight. There in the snow was a single red shoe. "Where would he have gone without his shoe?" she asked herself. "Even he wasn't drunk enough to be walking in this snow with one shoe. Besides, there are no footprints other than my own leading away from this spot."

But there was one other trail leading away. It wasn't footprints. It almost looked like a track that a ski would make. But only one ski. Could it be the track of a man's heel if he was being dragged backward? She followed the track past the dumpsters in the back of the parking lot. It continued into an alleyway behind the lot. She could hear a nauseating slurping sound emanating from the alley. Every fiber of her being screamed out at her not to look in there.

But she knew that she must.

In the alleyway she saw a scene of lunacy and horror. Shock transfixed her body. Three huge figures, each perhaps nine feet tall, stood at the far end of the alley. From her distance, Lena could not quite make out their facial features, but she had no doubt that they were not human. One held Kenny in mid-air with one-handed ease. The other was adjusting a tube that was hooked up to Kenny's neck. Through the clear tube she could see his blood being pumped from his body into some sort of backpack on the first creature's back. Kenny was still alive and was making feeble attempts to move his fingers and legs. She knew that momentarily he would be dead.

Lena watched as the first creature squeezed Kenny's neck tighter to speed up the blood flow. She saw the second creature continue making adjustments to the tube.

Lena saw the third creature...

The third creature was looking directly at Lena and began to charge!

Primal instinct took over as Merlena turned and ran for her life. She had about a thirty yard head start, but she knew that gap was closing fast. Her pumps had looked great on the dance floor, but were ill suited for a high-speed sprint through fresh snow. In mid-stride she kicked them off and darted barefoot back from the alley, past the dumpsters, and into the parking lot. The pursuing creature's footsteps were silent, but its powerful breathing was audible and getting closer. Lena knew that she would never reach the safe haven of the club. An instant later she felt an immense hand grab her by the back of the neck and yank her off her feet. Now, for the first time, she got a close look at the facial features of this monster. It was vaguely human, but sinister and demonic in all attributes. Its eyes were entirely black except for small red pupils. Its nostrils flared open and shut in rhythm with its breathing. The creature's most frightening aspect was its mouth. Huge yellow fangs, too large for the mouth to contain, dominated two rows of razor-sharp teeth. Brownish saliva dripped through thin, cruel lips. Its tongue suddenly darted outward in a lizard-like fashion and it tasted Lena's face.

Lena's instinct to survive prevented her from fainting. Instead, she hoped that this monster was male and that its physiology was similar to a human. With all her strength she gave it a terrible kick into where she hoped would be testicles. The expression on the creature's satanic face went from surprise, to anger, to rage. It reared her back and slammed her through the back window of a parked SUV. Glass shattered everywhere and Merlena lay momentarily stunned. As she lay in the rear of the SUV, she blindly reached for something, anything, to aid her. Lena's hand closed on a large triangular-shaped shard of the broken glass. She hid it in her hand as the monster pulled her out by her ankles and then closed its taloned hands on her throat. With her last reservoir of strength, Merlena drove the sharp glass into the foul beast's left eye.

It released a primal howl of pain as brown syrupy fluid began to ooze from the impaled orbital socket. The creature then dropped Merlena to raise both of its hands to its gruesome injury. Merlena ran as fast as she could through the remainder of the parking lot. She reached the nightclub, threw open the doors, took two steps inside, and then collapsed.

Three

Terry Loman had replayed the scene of carnage from the previous night over and over again in his head. Now he replayed it once again, this time for the benefit of Chief Roland Garnett. The Chief was now only two years away from retirement. He had joined the force in the 60's as a beat cop and worked his way up the chain of command through solid, dedicated service and two Medals of Valor.

Washington would be an amazingly complex city to supervise for any police chief. Like any other city its size, it had its fair share of crime. But being the capital of the country meant there were always marches, protests, events, celebrations, festivals, and of course, the most important politicians in the world. Garnett had worked traffic control for the route of the funeral procession of President John F. Kennedy. He had handled crowd control for the "I Have a Dream" speech by Martin Luther King. He had arrested violent protesters of the Vietnam War. In the 80's he was involved in the incarceration of a crack-addict mayor, only to arrange security at the mayor's re-election party a few years later. What a long, strange trip it had been. Chief Roland Garnett had handled it as well as anyone could expect.

But this was something new. First the discovery of a body murdered in bizarre and unique fashion. Then the equally bizarre attack on his morgue staff by a lone and apparently unarmed stranger. A single man who effortlessly crippled two others and then disappeared into the night.

When Terry had finished his account, the Chief had learned nothing more than he already knew from watching the security tapes of the previous night. "Damn it Terry!" Garnett pleaded; "I spent the last twenty-four hours in the hospital with the family of one of my men who will need to have his arm amputated. Have you seen your assistant? They're still digging splinters of shattered bone out of his face! Can't you tell me anything more about the bastard who did this?"

"I'm sorry Chief." responded Loman. "It was just so ..... wait I could see a little bit of blonde hair under his hood."

"Good Terry, what about eye color?" asked the Chief.

Loman looked away, then said "His eyes... I haven't said anything about them because you won't believe me. His eyes were blue, but they weren't right. I mean, I don't know how to explain it, but his eyes .....glowed."

"What the hell does that mean?" demanded the Chief.

"His face was shadowed by his hood, but his eyes gave out an eerie, blue glow. I can't explain it, but those eyes were scary as hell," answered Loman.

Chief Garnett was getting frustrated. Terry was proving to be a pathetic witness. Still, Garnett stayed outwardly calm and asked "Terry, you said he had an accent. What kind?"

"I never heard anything like it," answered Loman.

"Eastern European? Asian? Spanish?" asked Garnett. "Come on Terry, give me something!"

"Chief, I think I've heard every major accent out there. I'm telling you, this was so different from anything I've heard that I can't even tell you something similar."

The Chief was about to ask something else, when an excited patrol officer came running in. "Excuse me sir, we have a call that's a little crazy, but I think you should know."

"Go ahead," replied Garnett.

"Sir EMS is transporting a half-unconscious woman to the hospital who has been pretty badly beaten. She said she was attacked by a nine-foot tall monster," started the officer.

"Sounds like a junkie who pissed off her boyfriend," said Garnett.

"Sir, she said another monster was draining all of the blood out of her date."

Garnett and Loman looked at each other. *Another body with its blood drained?*

"Still sounds like a junkie, but officer, let's get to that hospital and meet this young lady. Have them take her to a private room where we can talk to her. Have them radio ahead with her room number." Garnett said.

Terry Loman watched them walk hurriedly out.

Chief Garnett was not the only one on his way to visit Merlena Bennett at George Washington University Hospital. Another figure had been listening intently on the police scanner that he'd stolen the previous night at the morgue. When the call came across of a battered woman claiming injuries from an attack by a monster that drained blood, the figure raced for the hospital. Now he perched on a rooftop across the street from Lena's hospital room and stared intently across the distance into her window.

He did not need to hear words to know what was being spoken in the room. Body language told him everything. As he sat on the snowy roof he watched as Lena's frustration mounted. The police clearly did not believe her. He could see her shock as they told her that they found no evidence of her monsters. No footprints, no blood, no dead body. They had only found her high-heel shoes, one man's red shoe, and a smashed rear window on a Lincoln Navigator. And though vandalism had decreased dramatically since the cold front had arrived, a smashed window was still a minor crime. The police tried to convince her to give up the name of the boyfriend or lover or pimp that had beaten her. They recommended that she go easy on alcohol since the hospital blood tests had shown some in her system.

When she told them to go to Hell, they instead went back to the Southeast Precinct.

Eventually, Merlena's concussion, pain medication, and exhaustion combined to force her into a deep sleep. Throughout her sleep she could not escape nightmares of the horrible face of the monster that had stared so cruelly into her eyes.

Despite lingering pain and burgeoning fear, Merlena checked herself out of GW Hospital the following afternoon. She had re-dressed into her tattered and torn dress and jacket from the previous night. She could only shake her head as she thought about her appearance. She'd left her apartment looking so sexy and elegant last night. Now she looked like a beggar.

The hospital pharmacy supplied her with some anti-inflammatories and some painkillers. From the lobby she called a cab. It pulled up surprisingly fast. Merlena got in and directed the cabbie to take her home. He turned around, looked at her shabby appearance, and demanded his fare up front. Lena was too tired to argue. She withdrew the money from her purse and handed it to him. The cab was surprisingly new and clean. She looked at the picture of her driver posted in the back seat. "Bob Smith," she read. *You can't get a more generic name than that,* she thought to herself. The cabbie was white, with dark hair trimmed in a crew cut. He had a thin mustache and goatee. Lena was glad that he'd made her pay up front. At least that way he couldn't run up the fare if she dozed off. The jerk wasn't going to be very happy with his tip though.

The snowy roads made the trip slow going. The falling snow had finally abated but the temperature hadn't risen high enough to melt any of that which had fallen. Multi-lane roads were cut down to half their capacity simply because the plows had nowhere to push the snow other than the right-most lanes. As the cab meandered slowly home, Lena forced herself to try to look logically at the events of last night. Throughout her Jamaican childhood Lena had heard tales of *Obeah* or evil magic. Ghosts, spirits, and demons were all part of the island folklore. But they couldn't be real. Could they? Of course not.

Maybe Kenny had slipped something into her drink. PCP or GBH or LSD? Any of those drugs could have caused her to hallucinate. But no - the hospital blood tests only showed alcohol. Maybe Kenny had given her some sort of weird head injury when they fought. Would that have caused her to hallucinate? These and a hundred other theories raced through her mind as they drove on, until finally, they arrived at her building. As she looked out the window of the cab, the four stories to her apartment never seemed so high.

Merlena got out, stiffed the cabbie on his tip, and headed to the entrance. Lena opened the door to the building and started up the steps. Why bother with the elevator? It was always out of service. When it was working, it sounded and shook as though it would break down at any moment. So instead, she continued up the steps. Her aching joints felt just like the squeaky floorboards sounded. After what seemed like an eternity, she reached the door to her apartment. She fumbled for her key, unlocked the door and stepped inside.

The apartment consisted of four rooms: kitchen, living room, bedroom, and bathroom. After locking the door behind her, she let her coat and dress drop to the floor and started to run the bath. Merlena put on some soft, smooth reggae on the bedroom stereo and then prepared a snack in the kitchen as she waited for the tub to fill. As she sliced and fried up some plantain, the delicious aroma reminded her that she hadn't eaten since Kenny had picked her up the night before. Plantain alone wouldn't do. She munched on the remainder of some cold chicken from the fridge and finished it before she knew it. She washed everything down with some juice and then walked down the short hall to check on the bath. She was too tired to even realize that she'd forgotten to shut off the burner under the frying pan.

The tub was almost full. Merlena removed her bra and panties. She wiped away some of the condensation from the mirror and looked over her injuries. Throughout a hard life in Jamaica, full of poverty and difficulties, she had managed to remain remarkably injury-free. Her body had always healed quickly from the minor ailments it had incurred. Despite the bruises and welts that now covered her neck, back and shoulders, Lena felt very lucky not to have suffered worse. But what was it that had attacked her? She shuddered as she thought once again of that horrible face.

Lena turned off the water and sank herself into the tub. She laid back, relaxed and listened to the sweet signature music of her country. As she closed her eyes, she could almost imagine that she was on the soft, white sands of the beaches of Montego Bay. Thoughts of clear skies, soft breezes, and the smell of ackee and plantain cooking in the distance floated into her mind. These serene thoughts were interrupted by the smell of the burning cooking oil that Merlena now realized she'd forgotten to turn off in the kitchen. *Damn,* she thought to herself.

Then a powerful hand shoved her head under the water and held it down. Lena began to drown!

Lena flailed her arms and legs wildly in her panic. Still she could not free herself. In the midst of her struggle, she looked up through the water from the bottom of the tub at the face of her attacker. Staring coldly down at her was the cabbie that had just dropped her off no more than half an hour ago. There was no time for Merlena to wonder how this man had gotten into her apartment or why he was trying to kill her. There were only a brief few seconds of air left in her lungs for Merlena to get her head out of the water. From under the water she punched with both hands at the head of the cabbie, but she could get no leverage and therefore no power behind her blows.

Merlena had one more desperate last chance. She shot both her arms out of the water and grabbed the cabbie by his ears. With sudden force she pulled his head into the tub with her. He was clearly surprised by this move. Since he was already leaning into the tub to hold down Merlena, he was pulled in easily. Now it was Lena who was the aggressor on top and the cabbie desperately trying to pull his head out of the water. But his head and short hair had quickly become slick from the soapy water. Merlena was losing her grip. Cabbie freed himself and then both sprang out of the tub and faced each other in the tiny bathroom.

"Why are you doing this?!!!" Merlena shouted.

Cabbie remained silent and took up a martial-arts attack stance.

"What do you want from me?!!" she tried again.

A sneer on Cabbie's face was his only reply. Then he attacked again.

The bathroom was small. The tub, toilet, and sink took up nearly all of the tiny room. Though Cabbie's first punch crunched into Merlena's jaw, the miniscule confines of the bathroom hindered Cabbie's deadly kicks, chops and elbow strikes. Instead, he could only try to wrestle Merlena down to the ground. But her naked, wet body proved difficult to hold. And her strength and determination made her even more difficult to overwhelm.

Quickly, Merlena broke free, turned, and ran out of the bathroom and was into the kitchen in four quick strides. Cabbie was one second behind her. That second, however, would prove costly for him. It gave Lena just enough time to grab the pan with the still-burning, hot oil from the plantains and splash it into his face. Cabbie screamed in pain as the oil sizzled into his eyes, cheeks, and lips. Lena then took the heavy, cast iron pan and smashed it into his skull repeatedly until he lay motionless on the floor of the kitchen.

Merlena sank to the floor. Her injuries were severe. Her battered body now included a fractured jaw.

A few days ago she was just a girl working hard to improve her life. Now her life had gone crazy. *What is happening?* she thought to herself. *Did this man really just try to kill me? Am I trapped in a nightmare? Am I dead and in Hell?*

No Merlena, she assured herself. *Keep it together. You are awake and alive and you need to call 911 right now.*

She slowly crawled across the kitchen floor to the small, round kitchen table. She steadied herself and sat her dripping, naked body into the chair. Lena almost laughed to herself. She realized that despite the battle that had just occurred in the bathroom and here in the kitchen, her tabletop lay undisturbed from the way she had left it before that life-changing blind date. The newspaper was open to the help wanted ads. Some junk mail and bills were off to the side, next to the phone. In fact, if it weren't for the unconscious body of an attacker on the floor behind her, she might be relaxing at this table right now. Instead, she tried to steady her jittery fingers to dial 911. Lena took a deep breath and dialed the 9. She dialed the first 1.

Then she was pulled away from the table by the now-conscious Cabbie. He closed his hands around her throat and squeezed with all his strength. Consciousness began to slowly drift away from Lena. Her resilient body had finally been pushed beyond its limit. No strength was left to resist. Surely the end would soon come.

But suddenly, Cabbie's fingers released her throat.

Lena looked up from the floor with what consciousness remained. She saw that a darkly dressed figure with strange blue eyes had lifted Cabbie from her. In one savagely quick movement he snapped Cabbie's neck and tossed aside the body. The figure then knelt beside Merlena and looked into her hemorrhaging eyes. Merlena was still too weak to move. She could only stare up into the strangely familiar, bright blue eyes and rugged face of the man above her.

"Do not fear me Merlena Bennett," he said. **"We have much to discuss."**

Merlena felt his powerful arms and hands lift her up and cradle her. He began to carry her away. She tried to speak but her shattered jaw was incapable of movement. His eyes would be the last thing she would remember before she finally surrendered to the sweet oblivion of unconsciousness.

Four

It is a common misunderstanding that the Pentagon is located in Washington. It is actually just farther southwest in Arlington, Virginia. The Pentagon was originally slated to be built in an area known as Arlington Farms. President Roosevelt, however, was concerned that the structure would block the view of the Capitol from Arlington National Cemetery. For that reason, he ordered it built about a mile away from the originally intended site, which is where it stands today.

Just south of the Pentagon along a stretch of Route 7 stands a lesser-known building of the Defense Department that was recently constructed. It is a six-story office building. Unlike other office buildings in the area, this one is not clearly visible from the highway. It is not adorned with any corporate logo or rooftop sign. In fact, it is almost camouflaged by its blandness. Black, one-way glass windows allow in light but not sight. The acres of woods that surround the building have signs posted on the trees everywhere which read:

TRESPASSING STRICTLY FORBIDDEN!

The tall, steel fence surrounding the parking lot is topped with razor wire. The rooftop has literally hundreds of antennae and satellite dishes of every shape and size imaginable. It is known by its top-secret employees simply as "The Tower." Office 213 in the Pentagon is eagerly awaiting a progress report to be called in from an office on the top floor of The Tower.

The details of that report are being finalized in a heated one-way discussion right now. Major Marshall Watson is livid, having just learned that he will have to report failure to the Pentagon.

"You sent one man to take her out??!!!" he screamed with venomous rage.

"She's a damn immigrant with no family connections in the entire country! She lives in the middle of the D.C. ghetto by herself!!! You could have sent in a team of ten guys with grenade launchers into that damn neighborhood and nobody would have looked twice!!!"

Watson was verbally blistering the ears of his Chief Operations Agent. The agent, like all of the elite assassins under Watson's command, was known, referred to, and addressed only by his code name. In this case, "Dagger."

Dagger had not been looking forward to reporting the unsuccessful assassination attempt on Merlena Bennett. Major Watson was never a pleasant man to deal with. Dagger had worked with Watson long enough to know that failure would not be tolerated. More than once, Dagger had been assigned to eliminate an agent that had lost the confidence of the Major.

Dagger had never questioned an assassination assignment before. Usually the reason was obvious. Dagger had slain drug lords, crime kingpins, foreign agents, and suspected terrorists. He had taken out witnesses, prosecutors, defense lawyers and even judges in trials that were potentially damaging to the government. When he had finally been promoted to his current post, he assigned out the hits to his personal team of agents.

But this assignment had been bizarre from the start. Why was Merlena Bennett targeted? As far as he could tell she was no threat to anyone. She was an ordinary young woman leading a rather boring life. But now, the agent assigned to kill her had been found dead in her apartment with his head nearly torn off and the rest of his body badly bruised, scalded and cut. There was no evidence to conclude that anyone other than Bennett had confronted the assassin. What happened in there? Where was the Bennett woman now? How had she killed and escaped from one of Dagger's best men?

All of these thoughts and questions ran through Dagger's head as he stood at attention and did his best to hold up to Major Watson's verbal onslaught. The intimidating Major's mouth was now less than an inch away from Dagger's ear as he continued "......and you send a damn white guy into an all black neighborhood ??!!!! What the hell is wrong with you?!!! Think none of the locals noticed that?! Now get the hell out of my office and do whatever is necessary to find this woman and **BRING ME HER HEAD !!!!!!**"

Dagger saluted, turned, and walked out just quickly enough to avoid the heavy, oak door that slammed shut behind him. A trickle of sweat rolled down his forehead. He knew that he had to find and kill Merlena Bennett quickly or the Major would surely make Dagger the target of the next hit. But finding Bennett had just become exceedingly more difficult now that she had been scared out of her apartment. Dagger would do the usual. His men would be assigned to airports, bus and train stations, and police stations. Others would be assigned to stake out the homes of any friends or co-workers who might take her in. Merlena Bennett would be found and Dagger vowed that he would indeed present her head to Major Watson.

Five

Soft, white light.

Warmth.

Comfort.

Peace.

So this is Heaven. Merlena hesitated to open her eyes. *What wondrous sights will I see? Will it be a vista of clouds? Or perhaps a choir of angels heralding my arrival?* Merlena, like nearly all Jamaicans, was a devout Christian. She didn't merely believe in God, Heaven, and Angels. She knew of their existence. There was no doubt in her mind. *So do it Merlena, open them. Open your eyes. Just a peek. Do it.*

She forced herself to open her eyes. First just a sliver, then slowly, slowly - open!

Hmmm. Either heaven has been greatly exaggerated or I'm in a very nice, but very Earthly bedroom. Merlena sat up and took in her surroundings. She was lying on a large bed. The headboard and footboard had elaborately carved designs throughout their mahogany surfaces. Four large posts rose from the corners of the bed and supported a silky white canopy. Luxurious white linens dressed the plump, oversized mattress. This was quite a large room. Perhaps 25x30 feet, perhaps larger. But no other furnishings were in the room. The walls and ceiling were all the same shade of pure white. There were no wallhangings or artwork of any kind.

Lena slid out from her sheets and stepped down gingerly from the bed, trying to be as silent as possible. She had been dressed in a long, flowing, white nightgown. She saw two doors, each on opposite walls. The windows in this room were glazed by the outer frost. No view outside would be possible. Lena realized that the light in the room was emanating from bulbs cleverly hidden behind the ceiling molding. She cautiously crossed the hardwood floor and approached the nearest door. Merlena pressed her ear to the door and listened closely. She could detect no sounds. In fact, Merlena realized that the only sound she could hear was the pounding of her nervous heart. Sweat broke out on her palms as she placed her hand on the doorknob. Milliseconds seemed like hours as she slowly turned the knob. **Boom - Boom - Boom** pounded her heart as she slowly opened the door ...and saw...

...an empty closet. Quite a large closet, and completely empty. A clothes rod ran down the left and right sides of the closet and a full-length mirror was anchored about ten feet away into the far wall. Merlena approached the mirror and examined her appearance.

Oh Dear God, she thought, *how long have I been here?*

Merlena saw that all of her injuries had healed. Surely it must have taken months for her battered body to have recovered so completely. No lacerations or contusions of any kind were visible. She vaguely remembered suffering a broken or dislocated jaw in her fight with her apartment assailant. But now she felt no lingering pain in either her jaw or any other part of her body. In truth, she felt fantastic. Her body felt energized and alert. Somehow, her fear of her surroundings began to melt away and she decided to seek out her host.

Lena exited the closet and crossed the bedroom to the other door. This time with only a little apprehension she tried the knob. It was unlocked. She opened the door and stepped out into a long hallway. To her left the hall stretched about forty feet, appearing to end at a well-lit stairwell leading downward. To her right the hallway ran at least thirty feet before it became obscured in darkness.

Merlena was almost sure that her host was benign. After all, her body was healed from her injuries and she was apparently not confined. Therefore, meeting this person or people, rather than escaping from them, was her goal. She turned left toward the lighted stairwell.

The hallway was lined on either side with large portraits in extravagant golden frames. Merlena saw that there must be at least eighty of them. Each portrayed a handsome young to middle aged man from the shoulders up. Some of the men were white, some black, most appeared racially mixed. As Merlena passed one of the portraits, she suddenly stopped. This face was hauntingly familiar. She carefully studied the painting of the light-skinned black man with a shaved head and a goatee. He had a large scar above his right eye and a thick, muscular neck.

Where have I seen you before? Merlena asked herself.

She slowly and gently placed her hands on the man's painted facial features that were tugging at distant memories in her mind.

Merlena concentrated hard, hoping to ignite her dim spark of recognition.

She almost had it. The memory was almost there. She could remember seeing that face smiling down at her many, many years ago.

He was....... *Wait! What was that?*

The unmistakable sound of approaching footsteps jarred Merlena back to reality. Someone was coming from the darkened, far end of the hallway.

Her choices were clear to her; Lena could run away from the individual advancing toward her or she could stand and face him. Merlena placed a great deal of trust in her instincts. This "intuition" was rarely wrong. Right now it reaffirmed to her that if her host had wanted her harmed, he would surely have done so during what must have been a long comatose period for her. Instead, he had apparently nursed her back to health. All of these thoughts ran through her mind in an instant and her decision was made. She turned and faced the man emerging from the shadows.

He was about twenty feet away when she recognized him as the man who had saved her from the attacker in her apartment. He was now in a dark business suit. His long, blonde hair was pulled back into a ponytail. He was of less than average height and size, but the contours of his lithe, muscular frame were evident even through his suit.

He stopped a few feet from her and each looked over the other for a moment until finally he spoke.

"Good morning Merlena. I am glad that you are well."

"Who are you?" asked Merlena almost in a whisper.

"My name is Tritos.

I know that you have many more questions for me other than my name. Please allow me to escort you downstairs where I promise that I will answer everything."

"Lead the way Tritos." Merlena softly replied. She felt no reason to fear him, but his emotionless face and strange voice were a little disconcerting.

Tritos offered his arm. Merlena took it and allowed him to lead her to the stairwell. As they descended the steps, Merlena began to get some perspective on the enormity of the mansion that she was in. The steps led down a lazy spiral into a luxuriously opulent greeting room. No expense had been spared in the furnishings, artwork, or fixtures.

As Tritos led her silently through several rooms, she could not help but gape at the lavishness that surrounded her. Merlena took it all in as best she could. One hundred questions or more arose in her mind as Tritos led her through the rooms, but Merlena chose to remain silent until they arrived at whatever their destination might be.

That destination turned out to be a cozy breakfast room. Colonial oak molding reached from the hardwood floors up to a height of about twelve feet, where it reached the ceiling along three sides of the room. Various floral oil paintings hung elegantly on the walls. One of several fireplaces Merlena had seen throughout the house burned lazily in a corner. The fourth wall of the room was composed from floor to ceiling entirely of glass. Despite some built up condensation, it offered a lovely view across snow-covered acres of ground to woods in the distance. On the far side of the room, a hallway led presumably to the kitchen.

A large, round, wooden table and four chairs sat in the middle of the room. Upon the table was a breakfast feast. Lena was astonished to see traditional Jamaican breakfast foods. Ackee, codfish, hot tea and fruit juice were present. Even island fruits like sweetsop, guava, mango and pineapple were sliced and arranged on a platter. Everything looked plump, juicy and delicious.

"The food...how did you know...where did you find...??" Merlena didn't know where to start with the myriad questions that she had.

"**You must be extremely hungry. Allow me to answer your questions over your meal,**" replied Tritos.

Merlena was suddenly aware of a ravenous hunger and eagerly sat down and complied. Tritos sat across from her.

"**What I am about to tell you will be very difficult for you to accept. You have lived your entire life believing certain truths, which I am about to shatter. I ask only that you hear me out until I am finished.**"

Tritos paused for Merlena's reaction. She drank deeply from a goblet of a delicious burgundy juice from a fruit which she had never before tasted. When she had drained the contents, she put it down and looked directly into Tritos' eyes.

"I think you know," Merlena replied, "my life has been turned upside down. I've suddenly seen and experienced things that I can't begin to explain. So believe me Tritos, I will give you every chance to explain it to me."

"Very well."

"The first thing that you must understand is that Earth is not the lone planet in the universe supporting intelligent life. There are actually countless inhabited worlds. Each is dramatically different from the other in terms of culture, heritage and tradition. Surprisingly, however, the physical characteristics between most of the populations are remarkably similar.

"Technological abilities between these worlds vary widely. Some planets are still in the Stone Age. They struggle to understand fire and communication. Other planets' peoples travel effortlessly throughout space and would view the greatest technological achievements of Earth as simple and primitive."

"The planet known as Maalogg falls into this latter category. They mastered interstellar travel centuries ago. The Maal were a peace-loving people, eager to expand their knowledge. Early expeditions to foreign planets resulted in fruitful and prosperous relationships.

"It was on just such a visit that a horrible mishap occurred.

A powerful physically and psychologically addictive substance was accidentally discovered. Due to their unique physical makeup, only the Maal experienced the effects of the drug. At first the Maal aggressively outlawed the substance. But as it worked its way into more and more of the home population of Maalogg, enterprising criminals recognized its profit potential and forcefully sought it out. These procurers of the drug became known by the slang term roughly translated as ... Harvesters."

"What made the drug so addictive Tritos?" asked Merlena.

"It causes...... enhancement... in the bodies of Maal males."

"You mean, um, like Viagra?"

Tritos paused and then smiled. Though he tried to hold back, he even allowed himself a short laugh.

Merlena realized that it was the first time she had seen him betray any emotion at all. She thought that it might be the first time he'd smiled in a very, very long time.

"Very different from Viagra. The entire Maal body changes almost instantly. Height increases by as much as three feet. Muscle mass is amplified by nearly three hundred percent. Teeth and nails lengthen, harden and sharpen themselves. Skin toughens and thickens. Reason is replaced by rage and an urgent need for more of the drug. Physical strength and killing capacity become unmatched."

"But this can't be true. Can it?"

"You have seen enhanced Maal, Merlena. You were attacked by one of three that are currently on your planet."

"The night of my date...but what were they doing to Kenny?"

Again Merlena looked inward toward her instincts. Somehow she knew Tritos was truthful.

"They were harvesting the drug."

"What drug dammit! They were vacuuming out his blood!"

"The drug of which I speak, Merlena, is adrenaline. Produced and secreted into the human bloodstream during times of intense stress and fear. The harvesters that you saw were causing that adrenaline to be produced. They then drained every drop of their victim's blood to be sure to get every drop of the adrenaline."

Merlena could only sit there stunned and shocked. She desperately did not want to believe any of this to be true. She wanted to awaken from this nightmare to find her world normal and plain once again. But she knew every word he had spoken to be true.

He continued, "Maal bodies are incapable of producing their own adrenaline. However, adrenaline is produced by hundreds of different humanoid races on many different planets. It is one of those physical similarities of which I spoke earlier."

"In an attempt to protect those planets' populations from Harvesters, the government of Maalogg tried to provide artificially produced adrenaline to its addicts. It proved a poor substitute. It seems as though adrenaline is only at its most potent when harvested from living organisms during bouts of intense fear."

"Maalogg then sent members of its military Special Forces to serve as Guardians to vulnerable planets to assist their populations in defending against the Harvester threat. This was only somewhat successful. Many Guardians continue to fight valiantly to defend their assigned planets. But defeating an enhanced Maal in battle is nearly impossible, and thus many Guardians have died in the effort."

"Still other Guardians have given in to temptation and have begun to Harvest from the very people that they were assigned to protect."

"What do they look like once the adrenaline wears off?"

"They look human in nearly all aspects. They can mix in very easily with Earthlings."

"How do you know all this?"

"Because Merlena..... I am Maal."

Merlena had given up on her breakfast. Tritos' story had captured her attention completely. She only now took a few bites to break an uncomfortable silence. Tritos had paused as though he expected Merlena to react to his revelation with shock or panic. Outwardly she betrayed no fear. Internally, however, she was reeling.

Life was not supposed to be this way. The sun was supposed to rise in the morning and set at night. A rock was hard and water was wet. And blood was not supposed to be an export to another planet!!!

Merlena absently took a few more bites of her now unappealing breakfast. More questions arose.

"So... the man you killed in my apartment, he was one of the Harvesters?"

"That man was most definitely human."

"Why was he trying to kill me?"

"I do not know."

"You said before, um, you said that Guardians were sent to each planet."

"Yes."

"Are you one of our Guardians?"

"I am the only Guardian assigned to Earth."

"Well, that was some awfully bad planning!"

"You must try to understand Merlena. Earth is so far away from any other populated planet. Most creatures in the universe are unaware of its existence. Even on a well-educated planet such as Maalogg, Earth is not on any charts. I was sent here only as a token gesture. No Harvesters were ever expected."

"So call in some backup!"

"I have already requested assistance from Maalogg."

"Great. When will they be here?"

"Approximately eight months from now."

"What the hell Tritos? Are they walking through the galaxy to get here? I thought you people were more advanced."

"They are not walking through a galaxy, Merlena. They are traveling through hundreds of galaxies. They are doing so at a speed that Earth's greatest scientists could not hope to comprehend.

"A simple trip to Mars would take Earth spacecraft over eight months. Maalogg is over ten thousand times that distance from Earth."

Despite his lack of emotion, Merlena realized that she had offended Tritos. "I'm sorry. I didn't mean anything.... have you tried to contact the police or the U.S. government?"

"Earthlings are too arrogant in their belief that they are alone in the universe. They would never accept the idea that aliens existed here. Anyone approaching the police with such a warning would be locked away for psychiatric evaluation."

"As for the U.S. government, that is another matter."

"The governments of a small number of other planets have secretly allowed Maal to harvest their people in exchange for advanced weapons technology. I fear that the United States government may have entered into such a pact."

"No! It can't be!"

"It is no coincidence that the Harvesting is taking place in Washington. If the Harvesters feared retribution, they would have chosen a country with a weak government. Instead they have chosen the capital of the most powerful country on Earth."

"But if this is true, what are you going to do?"

"I must perform my duty. I must defeat the three Harvesters."

"You can't do that alone. They'll kill you."

"Yes. Were I to face them alone I would surely perish. But I am hoping to recruit one key ally who may just help to produce victory."

"Who are you talking about?"

"You Merlena."

"You're crazy. I survived that attack by pure luck. Next time I won't be so lucky. Why would you even think that I can help you against these Maals?

"Because, Merlena..... You too are Maal."

Six

Dagger was becoming extremely frustrated. There had been no activity on Merlena Bennett's credit or debit cards. There had been no withdrawals from her bank account. There had been no sightings of her anywhere, including any local morgues. So just where the hell was she?

He had been sitting in his government-issued, black Ford Expedition staking out Bennett's apartment building for quite some time now as he pondered these thoughts. He'd had the engine turned off for about half an hour now, but the outer cold was quickly encroaching. Once again he turned the key in the ignition to run the heater full-blast.

As cold as it might have been, it was still an improvement from the glacial air at the start of this cold spell last week. The snow had stopped falling, and though it still covered the ground, Dagger could see that residents of this neighborhood were slowly resuming their outdoor activities. About a quarter of a mile down the street, three well-bundled souls stood waiting at the bus stop for the 1:00PM red line bus. Two enterprising boys had taken advantage of school closings to go door to door with their shovels to try to make some money shoveling walks. Many of the row-homes that they passed were boarded-up. Many others were dilapidated and falling apart. But the boys pressed onward anyway. Dagger watched as they intentionally made a very wide loop to avoid walking near a group of four surly-looking men standing on a street corner. Occasionally a car would pull up to these men. The driver's side window would roll down and money was exchanged for crack.

It's always the same, Dagger thought to himself as he observed the transactions. *White teens and adults drive from their suburban havens into neighborhoods like this to feed their addictions. Not even snow stops them. If the politicians and prosecutors ever grew a real set of balls, they would come down as hard on the whites doing the buying as they do on the blacks doing the selling.*

Dagger's SUV had been a subject of interest for these drug dealers ever since he had parked. Because the windows were deeply tinted, they had no clue as to the number or identity of the occupant or occupants. For some reason they were confident that he wasn't a cop. In between their drug transactions, they stared down the block toward the Ford, trying to decide what to do. Finally, one of them, after much prodding, started walking over to Dagger's location. The dealer was tall, maybe six-foot-six, and very skinny. He was dressed in sneakers, jeans and a very nice Redskins jacket, scarf and hat.

Dagger sat calmly as the dealer cautiously came over to the passenger side window and tried to peer in. Unable to see anything through the deep tint, he thumped his fist three times on the window. Dagger pushed the button to let down the window until it was fully open. He stared coldly at the dealer, who had leaned his head into the window.

"Watchu want whatchu need man?" asked the dealer.

"I want and need you to get your filthy ass away from this vehicle," Dagger responded calmly.

The dealer wiped his runny nose with his scarf and gave Dagger a generous grin. Several rotted out stumps of teeth gave away the cause of the man's speech impediment. "Ah know yu aint no cop. We dun paid aw protekshun munny to da cops dis monf. So whatchu doin here?"

Faster than the dealer's dim reactions could follow, Dagger whipped his hand into his jacket, produced a pistol, and aimed it squarely at the forehead of the man.

Drug dealers live a dangerous lifestyle. This dealer goes by the name of Lonnie. He had both received and dealt out gun violence many times in his career. A gun in his face had ceased to be an intimidating sight a long time ago. But Lonnie could recognize that this was no ordinary gun. He had no idea what purpose the tiny microphone on the butt-end could possibly serve. He would have been shocked to learn that it was part of a voice-recognition system that allowed only Dagger to fire the gun. He could also see that the magazine and barrel were specially adapted. Little did he know that these adaptations allowed this pistol to fire any caliber of rounds, including armor-piercing bullets. But the most intimidating feature of the weapon inches from his face was the long silencer and muzzle flash suppressor. Lonnie could recognize in an instant that this was a weapon designed exclusively for killing by a trained killer.

"Last chance crackhead. Get your ugly, smelly, diseased face out of my window and your bony waste of a body away from my vehicle," whispered Dagger.

Lonnie did not need to be warned again. He backed away two steps and then turned and ran. Not even the ice patches in the street or the piled up snow on the sidewalks could stop him from running faster than he'd ever run in his life. He ran past his partners at the corner and kept running until he was well out of Dagger's sight. The other dealers ran after him, half out of fear, half out of curiosity to find out what had just happened.

Dagger looked down at a five-inch TV monitor in his dashboard. The hidden cameras he had installed in Merlena Bennett's apartment still showed the apartment to be vacant. Once again he turned off the engine to save on the gas. The Ford had a hundred great gadgets, but it slurped up gas way too fast. The last thing he wanted was to make a run for a fill-up and not be here when Bennett returned. She had to come back here eventually. Everything she owned was still in that apartment.

Oh what the hell is this? Dagger thought to himself. Lonnie and his posse had returned, and now each was approaching with a weapon drawn. Two had 9mms, one had a Saturday night special, and one actually had an AK47 assault rifle. The few residents who had been outside now scurried for cover. Evidently gun battles were nothing new to this neighborhood. And, of course, there would be no police response to shots fired. As Lonnie had said, they had paid the police their protection money for the month. Still, Dagger smiled. This would be a nice distraction from an otherwise fruitless day.

The four men surrounded the vehicle. "Da only reason you not dead is cos we aint wanna put no bullet holes in dat SUV we bout to take from you!" shouted Lonnie. "You get out an give us dat fancy gun an we let you walk away!"

Dagger slowly opened the door and stepped out.

"Give up the gun moferfukker!" screamed Lonnie.

"Gentlemen," responded Dagger calmly, "look to your hearts."

"Wut the fuk is dat sposa mean?" asked Lonnie.

"It means, quite simply, look to your hearts. You'll find them on the left sides of your chests," said Dagger.

The four men clearly suspected some sort of trick, but the standoff continued until one of the dealers finally chanced a look down at his chest and shouted "Serious yo! Look at y'all chests!"

All of the dealers now immediately looked down to find a small red dot of laser light focused over their hearts.

"I'm sure each of you recognizes the laser sights from the snipers' rifles pointed at you from the rooftops," Dagger said. "I promise you that if you even sneeze, they will drop you where you stand."

A receiver built into Dagger's vest pocket broadcast his lead sniper's voice: "Awaiting instructions Sir."

Dagger touched a hidden button on his vest to activate his transmitter and replied "Hold your fire until further notice."

Lonnie's posse clearly knew that they were in over their heads. Despite the cold, each of them was sweating profusely. None dared move. Dagger relished in the droplets of sweat that he could see dripping out from each man's hat. This was going to be fun.

"I want each of you to slowly lay down your gun at your feet," ordered Dagger. Each of the dealers eagerly complied. Then, without needing to be told, each man raised his hands and looked to Dagger for further orders.

"You there, what's your name?" barked Dagger while pointing at Lonnie.

In a suddenly and surprisingly respectful voice the dealer responded "Lonnie, Sir."

"Left Foot!" ordered Dagger to his lead sniper. A millisecond later a silent high caliber bullet blasted through the center of Lonnie's left foot. A miniature explosion of blood, bone, and skin painted the surrounding snow. Lonnie shrieked in agony and crumpled to the ground. He began to cry. His posse still dared not move. They could not run, they could not fight or the rooftop snipers would make quick work of them.

"Get up Lonnie!" ordered Dagger.

"I can't man!!" cried Lonnie through his tears. "You took off my fukkin foot!!!"

"Get up or your left hand is next!" demanded Dagger.

Lonnie screamed out from the effort, but was indeed able to stand up.

"Now listen up, all of you." Dagger shouted out as he addressed the posse. "We're going to have a race." Dagger touched his transmitter button. "Sniper team!" he hollered.

"Yes Sir!" came the reply from at least four voices through the jacket receiver.

"Kill the last man to get out of my sight!" instructed Dagger.

The posse took off at sprinter speeds.

Lonnie ran as best he could but howled in suffering with each step of his left foot. The bullet had produced a three-inch diameter hole in the foot that was leaving a bright red bloody trail. The three other posse members would soon reach their corner and make the turn to take them out of sight. Lonnie tried to fight through the pain to run faster but began to cry as, one by one, his partners turned the distant corner and disappeared.

Lonnie could picture the sniper taking aim. Where was the red laser sight dot right now? The back of his head? The back of his chest? Spinal cord? Why hadn't they shot him yet? He was nearing the corner. Maybe twenty more steps. Blood still squirted from the ghastly wound in his foot. With each pulse it sprayed up and out. Each step in the snow washed the wound clean for a second until the next pulse slobbered it red again. Now ten steps until the corner.

Lonnie could picture many of the residents of this street peeking out from their windows enjoying the show. After all, Lonnie had turned this neighborhood into his personal territory. He controlled the drug distribution. He had cut a bribery deal with the cops to keep them out. He had recruited local youngsters as drug couriers. Anyone who had stood up to him, he'd intimidated or knocked off. There was no chance anyone would make a call to 911 for Lonnie's sake. Through his tears he wished for a cop to come rescue him but he knew that there was no chance.

Finally the corner. Still no bullet in the brain. Lonnie dared to slow down to take a glance behind himself. His soggy red footprints led back to Dagger, who was leaning on his SUV with his arms folded. Even at the distance of several hundred feet, Lonnie could see that Dagger was laughing. He had enjoyed the show. And apparently he had called off the shot.

Lonnie limped around the corner and disappeared.

Seven

"You lie!" was all Merlena could think to say.

"What can you tell me about your father?" asked Tritos.

"My father is none of your business." replied Merlena.

"What do you know of him?"

"MY FATHER IS NONE OF YOUR DAMN BUSINESS!!!"

For a few moments there was a silence that seemed to last hours. This was unmistakably a sensitive subject for Merlena. She got up from the breakfast table and began to pace. Tritos remained emotionless and waited for her to cool down. Merlena stared absently out the glass wall, across the field, into the distant woods. She was lost deep in thought. A tear came to her eye but she quickly wiped it away.

"You want to know what I can tell you about my father?" asked Merlena. "Absolutely nothing. He abandoned my mother and me when I was a toddler. I never heard from him again. Never a birthday card, never a Christmas present, nothing. I was too young when he left to even remember what he looks like. I've never even seen a picture of him. We were too poor to own a camera. My mother would never speak of him. I don't think he was Jamaican. Probably some damn tourist who wanted to have some fun with a naive, young island girl while he was vacationing. I guess he went back to his country. Eventually my mom met another man and had other children. That man helped raise me. But it wasn't the same. You can't expect him to love me as much as he loved his own children. I hate him, Tritos. I hate my father."

Despite her best efforts, Merlena found herself near tears again. "I mean I know sometimes relationships don't work out. Couples don't always stick together. But I mean how do you just abandon your child? I'm not saying I needed his money. We were poor but we never went to bed hungry. But maybe just once in awhile he could have come by. Even if it was just to give me a hug."

The tears finally came. "Damn it Tritos, why did you bring him up. I mean what does he have to do with anything?"

"His name was Kollos. He was assigned here as the Guardian of Earth prior to my arrival."

"Liar!" accused Merlena through her tears.

"You know that I speak the truth Merlena. You saw his portrait in the hall upstairs."

Suddenly it all came back. Long forgotten and repressed memories rushed upon Merlena like a roaring tide. She ran out of the room and retraced her path back to the stairwell. Without slowing down, she bounded up the steps to the hall of portraits. She stopped at the portrait of the man who had captured so much of her attention earlier. It was true. Despite being so young when he left, she could not deny this to be the face of her father.

His face was portrayed on this canvas as stern and serious. But Merlena thought back to those faint, but emerging reminiscences and she remembered that face smiling and joyful. Once again tears welled up in her eyes.

"He did not abandon you by choice," said Tritos softly.

Merlena hadn't heard him approach. He now stood behind her and continued.

"For years he guarded Earth with no sign of Harvesters. But his assignment here was a lonely one. He made use of the financial resources that we have established here to travel this planet to better educate himself about its varied countries. During one such trip, he met and fell deeply in love with your mother. It was for her that he commissioned the construction and furnishing of this mansion. Once your mother had secured her visa, he planned to bring her here and marry her. Her pregnancy delayed those plans, but Kollos was overjoyed at the news. He lived with your mother in Jamaica while construction continued here on this manor. He was there for your birth and the first early years of your life."

"But he received a distress call from a Guardian of another planet suddenly besieged by Harvesters. I am sure that it was a heart-rending decision for him to answer his call of duty. But he fully expected to return to you and your mother. In the months that it took him to reach the planet, the situation had become impossible. Over fifty Harvesters had taken root against a primitive, defenseless population. Still, Kollos did not turn back. He led a team of five Guardians against the Harvester hordes. The situation was hopeless from the outset, but your father was undeterred. One by one his team was killed in battle until he alone remained. He fought heroically and sent many Harvesters to their deaths."

"No Guardian has ever matched the ferocity and tenacity displayed in battle by your father. His heroism in the face of overwhelming odds has become legendary."

"What happened to him?"

"This hall honors Guardians killed in the line of duty."

Merlena had known the answer before asking the question. For some reason, she needed to hear it. She'd needed to know that after a lifetime of wondering and hoping, it was time to stop. Her father was dead. She felt guilty now for hating him all of these years. But now her hatred began to direct itself to those responsible for his death. "You said that I could aid you against these Harvesters?"

"Allow me to train you Merlena. The blood of the most heroic Guardian in Maal history courses through your veins. You have inherited his genetic code. Surely you've felt the force of your Maal genetics control your actions at times. Any child of Kollos, male or female, is born a warrior. You have no idea of the power of the untapped abilities hidden within you. Avenge his death. Fulfill your potential. Fulfill your destiny!"

Merlena finally turned away from the portrait and faced Tritos. Gone were the tears, her eyes were clear. Gone were the doubts and indecision, her mind was equally clear.

She gave him her answer.

"Let's get started."

Eight

Somehow Lonnie had made it back to his apartment. He was very thankful that it was on the ground floor. His foot was a bloody, pulpy mess. He knew that he was in a very difficult situation. If he showed up at an emergency room, the attending doctor would be legally required to report the gunshot wound to the police. The responding officers would discover that Lonnie had several outstanding warrants. So forget about the emergency room. But if he didn't get the bleeding under control, he knew that he would lose his foot.

Lonnie rolled a big joint of his best South American pot and lit up. He took a long, deep hit to prepare for the intense pain that he knew would strike when he attempted to remove his left sneaker. Heroin would dull the pain much better, but he needed to stay somewhat coherent to try to stop the blood loss. After a few more hits, he took one long, last toke and held his breath. He kept his mouth shut and let the smoke drift leisurely out his nostrils. Lonnie pulled his left foot up and rested it on his right knee. The shoelaces, once white, were now deep crimson. The soaking blood and snow had combined to make them wet, sticky, and too difficult to untie. Lonnie pulled a switchblade from his pocket and gingerly began to slice the shoelaces off. Finally the laces gave way. He spread the shoe apart and cautiously began to pull it off.

"AHHHHHHH!!" he screamed out and immediately abandoned the task. He punched the couch several times in reaction to the terrible pain. This couldn't be done slowly. Each second of moving the shoe was causing excruciating agony. He resolved that he would need to yank it off quickly. Lonnie took the shoe in both hands and closed his eyes. He took a few deep breaths and then counted to himself. *One........Two.......* **"Threeeeeaaahhh Haaaa uuuggghhh !!!!!!!"**

As much as it nearly made him faint from the pain, at least the sneaker was off. Lonnie looked at what remained of his foot. He would make no attempt to remove his sock. Crusted blood and fleshy tissue had become one with the once-white cotton sock. The hole in his foot was about three inches in diameter and was surrounded by exposed bone. Lonnie had no feeling in his toes. The sock veiled whatever damage had been done to them. Tears of torturous pain flowed freely as he crawled to the fridge to grab a bottle of whisky. He took a good long swallow as he lay on the dirty white tile of the kitchen floor.

Alcohol kills germs, maybe I should pour some in. He slowly tipped the whisky above his foot and let just a drop fall into the wound.

"YAAAAAAHHHHHH!!!!! FUCK THAT!!" he screamed out in absolute anguish. The alcohol had set the wound ablaze. Now Lonnie was breathing so heavily that he was nearly hyperventilating.

Warrants suddenly became unimportant. He still didn't want to bring an ambulance to his apartment. There were too many guns and drugs to hide. Lonnie decided to drink himself drunk enough to dull the pain and then drive himself to the hospital. It wasn't far. He could give a fake name and address and take his chances. He picked up his sneaker to attempt to put it back on. As he turned the sneaker upside down, two thin, brown objects rolled out. It took Lonnie a full minute to realize that those were two of his toes. He then screamed and passed out.

When Lonnie awoke, he had no concept of what time it might be.

A glance out the window showed that the daylight had passed some time ago. He guessed that it might be around midnight. He wrapped his foot in a T-shirt. He then picked up his blown-off toes and put them in his pocket with the naive hope that maybe they could be sewn back on. As he did so, he confirmed that his car keys were in his pocket, then he staggered to the door.

The streets were deserted. Local residents learned long ago not to venture out after dark. It was too easy to get caught by a stray bullet from a drug dispute. It was too easy to get shaken down for cash or a welfare check or social security check. Lonnie was largely responsible for making this street dangerous. This was his street. Through violence and intimidation he had become its king. But the king had lost his regal swagger as he struggled to make it step-by-step to his curbside parking space about a block away. Each of those steps left a gory footprint of fresh, warm blood. The car seemed so far away. Each agonizing stride seemed to last an eternity.

About a mile away, three Harvesters - one missing an eye - were seeking out prey. Despite their distance, they could smell the sweet adrenaline pumping out of Lonnie's foot. With a touch to the belts around their waists, they levitated several feet above the rooftop on which they had been standing. Then, with surprising speed, they darted through the air toward Lonnie's street.

Like sharks nearing a feeding frenzy, they followed the scent of their intended victim's blood. Each closing second made them lust more maddeningly for their prize. Closer and still closer they came until finally their prey was within sight.

If he was not slave to the anguish that racked his foot, Lonnie might have noticed the bizarre set of shadows cast by the moonlight as the three fearsome figures passed briefly overhead. He might have heard the soft, controlled landing of their immense bulk on the nearest rooftop above. But his agony blinded and deafened him to all of his surroundings except his car, which he was nearing ever so slowly.

Though the Maal pack was desperate to sate their gory thirst, they would not risk exposure through a foolish attack in the open. In a harsh, guttural language, they whispered amongst themselves a quick plan of ambush.

Lonnie was now a mere six or seven steps from his sleek, black BMW. *Almost there,* he thought, *almost there.* But above his head, a long, thin metallic coil was dropping down silently toward him. Lonnie had already taken his car keys out of his pocket. He pushed the remote to deactivate the alarm and activate the keyless entry. He then reached out for the door, when suddenly, something wound around his neck and yanked him violently into the air.

There was no time to react or to wonder what, how, or why. He saw the ground quickly becoming more distant. And as he choked and tried to work his fingers between the cord and his neck, his body was drawn up ten, then twenty, then thirty, and finally forty feet up to the roof. Along the ascent, Lonnie's body began to convulse as the noose tightened around his neck. His body thrashed about in a desperate attempt to stay alive. But as he reached the rooftop, he may very well have wished he was dead. The sight that met his eyes was not one that he expected to see until he was sentenced to what would surely be an afterlife in Hell. For he thought that surely Satan himself could not be more frightening than the three creatures who held him now. Swiftly, one turned him upside down and held him suspended in the air by his ankles.

Lonnie was paralyzed by an icy fear that quickly overwhelmed him. He looked up along the length of his body to see the powerful, demonic beast that held him as it looked back at him and laughed. The black, midnight sky and bright, full moon only served to enhance the terror of the sight. Lonnie wanted to scream out but couldn't. He wanted to beg for mercy, but couldn't. He wanted to die, but couldn't.

Yet.

As he watched, Lonnie could see a second creature remove one end of a flexible tube from the metallic backpack of the creature holding his ankles. The other end of the tube remained attached to the backpack. While grinning devilishly, it held the tube in front of Lonnie's view and pushed a button on its side. Immediately a thin needle extended out and began to writhe, almost as if it were alive. To Lonnie, it almost appeared to be some sort of chrome earthworm. As Lonnie stared, the tube was fiercely thrust into his neck. There was a moment of pain, then Lonnie felt the needleworm squirm about in his neck as it sought out a major vein or artery. Lonnie began to shiver uncontrollably; not from the frozen night air, but from the maddening horror that engulfed him. He could feel the blood leaving his body through the tube. The needleworm was expanding to prevent the blood vessel from collapsing as it vacuumed out his lifeblood.

One last look up at his captors showed Lonnie that they were feverishly unwrapping his wounded foot. They returned Lonnie's gaze and flashed him triumphant, Satanic expressions of glee. Then their long, forked tongues began to lap up the blood oozing from the wound. Finally, Lonnie regained enough control over himself to be able to scream. He tugged desperately on the tube in his neck but it could not be removed. The screams of terror soon changed to shrieks of madness. They echoed through the street until finally the shrieks, along with Lonnie's life, came to an end.

Nine

Merlena's sword whistled through the air to block Tritos' thrust. Again and again their swords met in mid-air with a loud clang. They had been at this most of the evening and now late into the night.

A few hours ago, Tritos had led Merlena to the basement of the manor. Stone steps led down approximately thirty feet to a well-lit, massive gym. On all sides it stretched out into a cavernous, wide-open space. Occasionally, stone pillars wrapped in padding stretched to the ceiling about twenty-five feet overhead. Strange weapons, large and small, hung here and there in brackets along the perimeter walls. Those walls also featured padding from the floor to a height of about six feet. That padding was identical to the padding wrapping the columns. Rubber flooring was installed underfoot. It looked very much to Merlena like an immense martial arts studio.

The protective gear that they would be wearing was introduced to Merlena. Tritos showed her a black, quilted top and pants. To Merlena it looked not much different than standard athletic sweats. But Tritos explained that this Maal fabric, called Slissen, was far stronger than Kevlar. It was impervious to nearly any bullet or blade. The quilting beneath the Slissen was composed of another Maal textile called Camac which was very effective at absorbing the force of incoming blows. It therefore considerably reduced the power of their impact. When Merlena put on this exotic armor, she was surprised at how light and soft it felt. It was not much different than normal clothing. Tritos helped her don a neck guard of the same material and finally she put on Slissen gloves and a protective helmet.

Tritos then changed into his own gear. Merlena caught herself allowing her eyes to linger a bit too long when he removed his shirt. He was slender, but every muscle was sculpted to slim, masculine perfection. She found herself blushing and was relieved that his Slissen pants fit overtop of the trousers that he was already wearing. His armor was identical to that which Merlena wore, though he stopped short of wearing a helmet so that it wouldn't muffle his voice as he instructed her.

Tritos had decided to begin Merlena's training with swordplay. He had started her off gently at first, with bamboo swords. But he was amazed at how fast she learned basic and then advanced kata. Within a matter of hours she was ready to move on to solid wood and now metal swords. Merlena was astonished at these latest weapons. Tritos had handed her something that appeared to be similar in size and shape to a flashlight. At his direction, Merlena held it in her hand and applied a firm grip.

Immediately, a four-foot blade extended from the top of the unit. Two smaller blades extended up and then to the side until it formed a beautiful broadsword. Tritos had explained to her that it was forged on Maal of a metal called Orem. It was stronger than steel, yet lighter than aluminum. Because it could retract into such a small size, it was an excellent weapon to carry on one's belt. Merlena was amazed at the sharpness of the blade. She was able to shear through boards and even cinder block with effortless single strokes. The only thing that she had encountered capable of withstanding her sword had been Tritos' Orem blade.

Now, as they sparred back and forth, the sword began to feel almost as an extension of her arm. Her movements were graceful and accurate. She could almost sense his strike before he made it. Although Tritos was not engaging her with full speed, he was impressed nonetheless.

"The sword is natural to you," he said. "Your father's genetics are strong in you. Tutelage isn't needed so much as repetition to improve your skills."

"I feel good about my defense," replied Merlena between strokes. "I'm just not sure how to strike at you without leaving myself wide open." Her voice was muffled by her helmet, but Tritos' hearing was more sensitive than any human's ability.

"Relax. Let your instincts guide you." Clang after clang sounded as their swords continued to come together. Tritos spoke louder to be heard above the din. "Cease looking for an opening. Allow the flow of my attack to reveal the opening for you."

Merlena tried to relax. Gradually she could begin to see patterns to his movements. What seemed like random strikes at first, now began to take on order. She watched not only his sword, but also the movements of his wrists, arms, and shoulders. Even his eyes revealed split-second hints to the direction of his motion. She began to feel more and more of the genetic influence of her father. Fighting was not a learned skill for Maal warriors. It was an inherited trait.

Long dormant instincts were awakening. Merlena began to feel less reliant on reflexes and allowed her instincts to control her body and the Orem Sword. She saw an opening in Tritos' defense a split-second before it actually occurred. Instantly she attacked with a mighty slash aimed at the protective guard around his throat. But before it could reach its target, Tritos ducked beneath her blade and swiftly brought the point of his own sword up gently against her abdominal armor.

Merlena threw down her sword in anger, tore off her helmet and blurted out a few choice Jamaican curses. She had always hated to lose in any competition.

"**Your skills are truly amazing,**" complimented Tritos.

"I'd be stabbed in the belly just now if this were a real fight," replied Merlena. "So don't call me amazing."

"**You had a sword in your hand for the first time this evening. I did not hold much back, yet you nearly bested me. You will improve exponentially in a very short time.**"

"Enough with the swords. We're not gonna get into close combat with these creatures anyway. Where are the laser guns?"

"**We shall not battle the Harvesters with guns.**"

"What are you talking about? Why not?"

"**It is cowardice to kill one's enemy from a distance. It is not our way.**"

"It'll be my way. I've seen these things close up. Trust me, I have no issues taking these things out from a distance."

"**It saddens me to hear you speak in this manner. But I must remind myself that you were raised on a planet where war now can take place between countries continents away from each other, with neither side setting foot on the other's soil. Commanders of Earth's great armies of the past would personally lead their troops into battle. Today they simply push a button that can launch missiles to kill thousands or even millions. There is no honor in that. It is pure weakness. If the...**"

"If the ancient Romans or Vikings or whoever else you're thinking about had guns, they would've used them. Even you can't match the Harvesters strength or speed. We need an advantage."

"**Our training and planning shall be our advantage. Leave the handguns to the criminals and miscreants. Even the most crazed Harvester would not resort to a gun. We shall defeat the Harvesters honorably. As I said, in time...**"

"There is no time Tritos!" interrupted Merlena. "How many will die tonight? How many? There are three of them out there killing every night. How many more nights until we do something?"

"**We are doing something. Your further training is vital. But you must not try to rush through it.**"

"We don't have time to train me in hand-to-hand combat. These things need to die!"

"They are not things."

"What?"

"They are not things. They are Maal, just as are you and I. They are not insects or rodents to be killed without a second thought. The killing that they do is motivated by an addiction out of their control."

"Are you telling me that you feel sorry for them? Do you have some kind of sick respect for them?"

"It is not the Harvesters that I respect. Regardless of their addiction, they are killers who will not stop until they themselves are killed or apprehended. However, I do respect our ability to take away life. I shall not do it in a thoughtless and cowardly fashion. I shall defeat them in honorable combat."

A long silence followed. Merlena paced back and forth, deep in thought. "I don't think I can do this Tritos," she said. "I'm not a warrior. I'm just a regular girl. This isn't the movies. Shooting them would have been so much easier. I don't think I could kill anything with my hands, not even a mouse."

"I understand your fear," replied Tritos.

"I didn't say I was afraid."

"No...... you did not." After a moment Tritos walked softly over to where Merlena stood with her back to him. He put his hands gently onto her shoulders. "But only a fool would not be afraid."

"It is possible that one or both of us may die from the battle that we shall soon undertake. But it is certain that many more shall die if we do nothing."

His strong hands and calm voice restored courage, hope, and faith in her soul. And though some doubt still lingered, Merlena fought it off. She stepped over to where her discarded helmet lay and placed it back upon her head. She then picked up the Orem sword, which had retracted back into its handle. After a moment of thought she gave it a firm grip. Once again the beautiful blades extended to form the imposing broadsword. Merlena held it aloft and admired the deadly beauty as the overhead lights glinted off the side of the nearly four-foot-long blade. She flexed, then relaxed the muscles of her arms and shoulders. She then stretched her neck around to intentionally crackle some vertebrae.

Merlena looked over at Tritos and said, "What are you waiting for? We have training to do."

In a rare display of emotion, Tritos allowed himself a broad smile. Merlena couldn't resist a sarcastic reply.

"Careful now Tritos, you'll change my entire impression of you if you actually show some personality."

Tritos immediately changed back to the serious expression that seemed sometimes permanently affixed. **"Prepare to defend yourself."**

Once again the swordplay resumed. As the night wore on, Tritos would occasionally call out instructions, but that was becoming far less necessary. Merlena's inherited traits made her a natural at combat. She moved as one with her sword. The fighting was almost taking on the grace of a choreographed dance.

It was also becoming more ferocious. Tritos still didn't unleash his full offensive load upon her. But he soon found it necessary to be at his defensive finest to hold back Merlena's attacks. Quicker and quicker the swords darted through the air, forming a blur of lethal movement. Tritos now was silent as he put his full concentration into his actions. His instructions were now unnecessary. Merlena was in a zone where thought, movement, strategy, and skill had all blended into instantaneous action. Her inherited Maal abilities had finally fully awakened and taken over all Earthly control of her mind and body.

She saw the opening in his defense well before it occurred. After all, she had used her last seven moves to set it up. Her strike was immediate. Her sword slashed across Tritos unprotected face, slicing a ghastly wound into his cheek, nose, and eyebrow. Blood poured out instantly. Although there are no major blood vessels in the face, so many had been opened that the bleeding was significant. Tritos was silent as his hands flew up to his face and he sank down to his knees, but it was obvious that he was in intense pain. The sight snapped Merlena out of the almost hypnotic state that she had entered during the combat.

"Oh my God, Oh my God!" Merlena began to panic. "Jessum Priest, why didn't you wear a helmet?!"

Tritos was kneeling down with his face buried in his hands on the floor. Merlena was crouched over him with her hands on his back, unsure what to do. He hadn't attempted to lift his head, so she still hadn't seen the wound. But she knew that it was severe from the amount of blood that was gushing through his fingers and pooling on the floor.

Finally, while still hiding his face, he raised a bloody hand to point at the far wall. **"In... that cabinet..... is a container filled with a burgundy nectar. Bring it....... quickly."**

Merlena ran to the cabinet and threw open the door. The interior was climate controlled and contained at least sixty clear glass bottles. All appeared to be filled with the "burgundy nectar" Tritos had described. There were no markings on the bottles, they all looked the same to Merlena. She wasn't sure if he needed a certain one specifically.

"Which one dammit!?" she shouted in a panic.

"**Aиц,**" responded Tritos calmly but feebly. He was still cradling his face in his hands and hadn't risen from his knees.

Merlena raced back with a bottle and twisted off the lid, which had been sealed with some sort of wax. A powerful, fruity aroma rose to her nostrils. She immediately recognized this as the wonderful juice that she'd enjoyed along with her breakfast this morning. Tritos extended out his hand for the juice and rose unsteadily to his feet. Now Merlena could see the full extent of his injury. It was a gruesome sight to behold. Her single sword stroke had begun its contact at the lower portion of his right cheek. It left behind a large enough slice to expose his teeth. The blade had apparently traveled upward across his nose and left the nose attached to his face only by the skin and cartilage closest to the nostrils. But the worst injury caused by the blade was the area above his left eye. The entire flap of skin containing his eyebrow had been partially severed and had peeled down and was now hanging over the eye. Luckily, his eyeballs themselves were spared any goring. But they emanated a bright blue, phosphorescent glow. Merlena now recalled seeing that same radiating blue glow in his eyes the very first time she had ever seen him, back when he saved her from the attack in her apartment. The severity of his injuries, however, overruled any curiosity she might have had over what unique feature of the Maal physiology might cause the emanation of color from the eyes.

"My God Tritos, I... I'm sorry. We need to get you to a hospital. Oh God."

Merlena was worried about the severity of the wound. At best it was disfiguring, at worst it could very well prove fatal. But as Tritos raised the bottle to his lips and drank lustily, Merlena watched an amazing thing happen. The wounds began to heal themselves. Merlena stood transfixed with awe as she watched muscle fiber and tendon regenerate and fuse previously separated tissue. Tiny nerves, veins and arteries that were severed gradually reconnected and instantly healed. Cartilage and then skin renewed itself right before her eyes.

His nose and eyebrow, which had been so mutilated, were nearly finished restoring themselves. As this astonishing healing occurred, the deep blue glow in Tritos' eyes slowly dimmed and finally extinguished itself.

Tritos had drained about half the bottle. He took it away from his mouth and poured a little on his hand. He then dabbed the juice on his face with that same hand. A moment later there were no remaining signs that he had ever been injured. Only the warm, platter-sized pool of blood on the floor betrayed any sign that there had ever been an injury.

Tritos held out his open hand. Merlena placed her own inside it. She stared incredulously at the once-again handsome face that had been so gruesome mere moments ago.

"Thank You," said Tritos.

"What.... what just...... what.."

Tritos helped her finish the obvious question. **"What just happened?**

The nectar is that of a prized Maal fruit that we call Elsperium."

"Elsperium?"

"Correct. As you have just witnessed, its healing properties are quite considerable."

"Quite considerable? Try amazing. That's a miracle. Can it heal anything?"

"Not quite. It is ineffective against viruses and bacteria. That makes it important to administer to wounds prior to the onset of infection. And though it can heal tissue, it cannot completely replace it. For instance, if a toe or finger, or in tonight's case, a nose had been amputated, it could not re-grow. But as you said, it is an amazing healer."

Merlena just now realized that Tritos had continued to hold her hand during his explanation. But that was just fine. It felt good.

"It played a large part in your healing process after I brought you here. The Human portion of your physiology slowed the process slightly, but you still greatly benefited. Your recovery might otherwise have taken months, and even then been incomplete. Instead you have taken less than a full week to heal."

Before tonight, she could never have believed that she'd been here only a couple of days. Up until this very moment, Merlena had thought she'd been here for at least a month. She remembered how severe her wounds had been. *Less than a week! Amazing how much my life has changed in less than a week,* she thought to herself.

Still holding his hand, Merlena led Tritos over to a wooden bench adjacent to the far wall. They sat down.

"When I first saw you, you know, in my apartment, when you saved me from that attack? Anyway, I thought I remembered seeing a weird blue light in your eyes. Up until now I thought that maybe I dreamt it. But when you were injured just now, I saw it again."

"That is a part of Maal physiology which you have apparently not inherited. Strong emotions trigger a chemical reaction in our orbital fluids which cause the emanation of color from our eyes. Was it blue that you saw?"

"Yes, exactly."

"Blue is a sign of intensity. Such intensity can be brought on by the competition of battle or the struggle to control pain. Other emotions, when strong enough, can cause other colors to arise. Rage, for instance, causes red. Grief will cause green."

"That is totally bizarre."

"Is it? Personally I find human eyes even more bizarre. They do not emit color from strong emotions; instead they leak water. You call them tears. Human tears can be caused by everything from joy to sadness to pain. Is crying really any more logical than color emanation?

"I guess I never thought about it that way."

"I think you should get some rest. We have a long day of training ahead of us tomorrow."

"Do you sleep?"

"After this sword fight with you, I shall sleep very well indeed," said Tritos with a smile.

He led her back up the stone steps to the main floor. They passed through the manor, and eventually reached the grand staircase leading up to the sleeping quarters. As they walked, Merlena began to realize that she was developing feelings for Tritos. It was more than just the security and safety that she felt with him. She was starting to feel a bond with him that she'd never felt with a man before. Though they'd only just met, and had done so under uncanny circumstances, she recognized a very special feeling welling up inside of her.

As they passed through the corridor of heroes, Merlena paused once again at her father's portrait. She kissed her fingers and then pressed those fingers to Kollos' painted lips. Tritos put a comforting arm around her shoulder and after a moment they arrived at the doorway to Merlena's bedroom.

"Rest well Merlena," said Tritos. **"Tomorrow you learn to fly."**

"Excuse me?!"

Tritos responded only with a smile. He turned and walked away down the hall.

"Rest well."

Ten

Viewing murdered corpses was never a pleasant task. But this body was especially unsettling. Every time that Terry Loman began to think that his many years as a coroner had desensitized him, he came upon a cadaver that brought new revulsion. The body that lay on his examination slab tonight was in typical autopsy position. It was lying on its back with both arms straight against its sides and both legs even and in line. But it was the position of the head that caused such a ghastly sight. The neck had been forced into a complete 180-degree twist until the head actually faced backward. Loman was staring at the front of the corpse's body, but the back of its head. That head had been twisted so violently that it had nearly been torn off. Only what little skin and muscle remained intact within the neck kept the head and body attached.

Where to start, where to start? Loman thought to himself. He ran a hand through his thinning, curly, gray hair and squinted through his bespectacled, tired eyes. Loman then donned a surgeon's mask and gloves. He pulled down the large, overhead examination lamp and turned it on. Its white bulb and reflective dome cast an even brighter light on this grisly sight. He then pulled down a microphone from the same fixture to record his verbal notes. The autopsy would also be filmed. Videotaping of all rooms in the morgue was now done twenty-four hours a day. That had been started as a result of the attack by the still unknown assailant that hospitalized Loman's assistant and guard. Terry still shivered when he thought back to that night. He forced himself to place those unpleasant thoughts aside and return to the unpleasant task at hand.

"Unknown Caucasian male," he announced into the microphone. "Approximately thirty-five years old."

He continued with a brief summary of the crime scene. "Found murdered in apartment 441 at 1781 South Tuxent Street. Name on the rental agreement for said apartment is Merlena Bennett. Neither Bennett or any other subjects were found in the apartment with the body."

"No obvious tattoos, permanent scars or birthmarks," Loman continued. "General description of wounds is as follows: moderate blunt force trauma to shins, ribs, arms, shoulders, and head. Severe burns to the face. Severe, uhhh, extremely severe trauma to the neck."

Loman continued, " Specific external injury description is as follows: Moderate contusions to, and evidence of, hemorrhaging from the temporal, occipital, and femoral lobes of the cranium and brain. A one-inch diameter indentation caused by a blunt edge is evident just behind the right ear. No......... wait, there are more."

Terry ran his gloved fingers through the cadaver's hair feeling for more of the curious indentations. He used both hands and could eventually feel six, then eight, then finally a total of ten. The fingers and thumbs of Loman's hands fit almost perfectly into the indentations that had been forced into the cadaver's skull.

Jesus, Terry thought to himself, *Someone's bare hands crushed these creases into this man's head!*

The human skull is soft at birth. It is composed of separate plates which will not fully fuse together for several years. This is necessary to allow the skull to flex and contract as it is squeezed through the birth canal during delivery. However, once those plates do fuse in early childhood, they form a formidable armor for the brain known as the cranium. Nature could not have devised a better design for the shell that protects the body's most important component. The cranium expands as the body and brain grow larger through childhood and adolescence. All the while it grows stronger into adulthood, protecting the precious brain from severe injuries. Terry Loman could not fathom any human being who could possibly have the strength of grip to do much worse than bruise the outer surface of the cranium. Yet this corpse clearly had two handprints crushed into its cranium. The evidence was undeniable.

His trained mind was already theorizing a murder scenario. *The killer came upon the victim from behind and took a firm grip upon his head. This grip had superhuman force. With equal force, the killer then twisted the head, severing the spinal column and nearly beheading the body.* It would be an entirely implausible theory if the clear proof was not lying here before him.

Loman thought back to the amazing speed and strength of the stranger that attacked his staff here and shivered. *Could this be a victim of that same man?* Terry nervously cleared his throat and announced his findings on cause of death into the microphone. There would be much more to do to continue the autopsy, but Terry turned his attention toward trying to identify the body.

No wallet, driver's license, or documents of any kind were found on the body at the crime scene. A cab was found parked behind the apartment building, but it turned out to be stolen. The placard in the back seat of the cab proclaimed this man to have been "Bob Smith." But the name, and the placard, were fakes. *So just who are you?* Terry silently wondered.

He began the identifying procedures. Later, he would x-ray and mold the teeth to check them against dental records. First though, it was time for fingerprints. Identifications through fingerprints were so much easier these days compared to when Terry had first started out in the Seventies. Technological breakthroughs in computer capabilities, and more importantly, in communication were a coroner's dream come true. The D.C. Police network, like most of the precincts around the country, is tied into a Federal database of literally millions of fingerprint files. To find a match, Terry needed to merely get his cadaver's prints, scan them into the system, and allow the computer to do the rest. If this man had ever been arrested, served in the military, worked certain positions in the government, or been involved in several other scenarios, his prints would be on file. To begin this process, Terry reached over to the stainless steel, rolling storage cabinet at his side. From the middle drawer of the seven on the cart, he produced his inkpad and templates. He started with the right index finger, grasping it in his hand and pressing it firmly into the black ink. He then rolled it perfectly onto its framed area on the template. He always liked to check each print before moving to the next, just to make sure there were no smears or blotches. But something was very wrong here, and smears and blotches weren't the problem. There was no print!

Only a smooth, black patch showed on the paper where the finger had been placed. Loman quickly grabbed both of the corpse's hands and flipped them over. There were no fingerprints on any of the fingers. Only coarse, flat, scarred skin.

Memories from more than thirty years ago suddenly came back to Terry. During his field service in Vietnam, Terry remembered a story that another medic had confidentially told him one night in their tent during a lull in fighting outside of Qui Nhon. *What was his name? Norm... Norman Mason. Yeah that was it - Norm Mason.*

Norm Mason had told Terry that he'd been stationed at a M.A.S.H. unit far in-country. Mason had been serving as acting officer in charge since the recent death of their lieutenant. Late one night, a Special Forces unit of ten Green Berets arrived at the camp unannounced. All of the men appeared to be of Asian ethnicity. Mason was called in to meet with their commander and ordered to use hydrochloric acid to burn off the fingerprints of the Green Beret team. He was not given a reason for the procedure and ordered to secrecy. Mason reluctantly carried out the bizarre order. After applying the acid bath to the soldiers' fingertips, he carefully bandaged them and advised their commander to allow them to rest for at least a week to let a layer of skin grow over their bare flesh. During that week, Mason kept careful watch over the team. Infection was a big concern, and their bandages needed changing frequently. Their commander would allow no medic other than Mason to attend to them or even see them during their stay.

One night, one of the Green Berets snuck into Mason's tent while he slept. He gave Mason his dog tags and the phone number of his mother back in the States. He whispered to Mason that they were about to attempt to assassinate the leader of Cambodia. The leader's potential successor had secretly indicated a willingness to allow the U.S. to conduct operations from within Cambodian borders. This would be a huge advantage for American forces. Their fingerprints had been removed, so that if the mission failed and these men were killed, they could not be positively identified as Americans. The man said that if he lived through this mission, he would contact Mason within the next few months. If he didn't, he begged Mason to contact his mother after the war and let her know his fate. Norman Mason agreed.

Before hearing the story, Terry had shared at least half a dozen joints with Mason that they had snuck into their tent. Mason got so wasted, he probably never remembered telling the story. The next day Terry was sure that he had imagined the story or that his colleague had made it up.

But right now it seemed very real.

It was not unheard of for a criminal to attempt to deform or mutilate his own fingerprints. Permanent scarring or acid-burning were favorite techniques. But the job done here was professional from start to finish. Replacement skin from another area of the body may have even been surgically grafted onto the fingertips.

Was this man also a member of some secret government team? Terry asked himself. *How else can the absence of fingerprints be explained? What was he doing in the Bennett woman's apartment? And who the hell killed him?*

Though he had a very strong feeling that it would be fruitless, Terry decided to pursue identification through dental records. He opened the mouth of the cadaver to examine the teeth. Not surprisingly, there were none. No real teeth anyway. Terry removed the dentures from the cadaver's mouth and examined them under magnification. No serial number, no traceable information whatsoever was engraved on them.

Surrendering for now his attempts to uncover an identity, Loman resumed the autopsy on the body that would be logged in and stored as John Doe #17967. It would prove to be an autopsy that would run through the remainder of the night and into the early morning hours. Many more questions would arise.

All of the questions were disturbing.

Loman was sure that none of the answers would be comforting.

Eleven

The sunrise in Potomac was beautiful this morning. Merlena paused for a moment to admire the many shades of red, pink, auburn and violet that painted the sky. For a moment it was almost possible to forget the inconceivable truth that alien drug lords had come to Earth to harvest Human blood from terrified, unwilling donors. In that same moment, she tried to forget that she was in rigorous training to wage mortal combat upon these aliens. She sat back and relaxed here on the frozen veranda behind the manor. The frost of her exhaled breath wove gently in the air with the steam from the cup of hot tea that she was slowly sipping.

Merlena's Slissen and Camac suit kept her remarkably warm despite the raw morning air. This was the first time since arriving that she had gotten a good look at the acres of ground surrounding the manor. As far as she could see, an open field surrounded by undisturbed woodlands stretched outward. In the distance, a small pack of deer foraged. High above, a hawk circled regally in the sky. Her present surroundings were in stark contrast to the congested, confining streets of the city. Merlena had never truly adapted to the bustling, hurried streets of Washington. But despite being a close suburb of the nation's capital, Potomac seemed a world away.

She allowed herself to snap out of these brief, tranquil thoughts upon hearing Tritos approach. He too was dressed in the black, Slissen suit, though he also wore a large, thick, black belt with an unusual buckle. It reminded Merlena of the weightlifting support belts that she'd seen bodybuilders wearing. Over his shoulder he carried another, identical belt, and this he handed to Merlena.

"What's this?" she asked.

"Call it a Levitation Belt. As I told you last night, you will be learning to fly today," replied Tritos.

"Yeah, I thought you meant a helicopter or a jet, or even a flying saucer. What's with the belt?"

"Please, put it on."

Merlena did as he asked. After buckling it, she thought she felt a momentary tingle run from her belly to her brain, but it was immediately gone and she gave it no further thought.

"The Belt," Tritos explained, **"uses a technology that works against the natural gravity of the earth. Similar to magnets of the same polarity, it actually repels the wearer against the gravitational source."**

"So how does it work?"

"It responds to your mental commands."

"What do you mean?"

"Think up."

"Huh?"

Tritos smiled, or was it a smirk? Then he simply pointed up into the air and repeated **"Think ......up."**

"Merlena looked upward into the peaceful, azure sky and its soft billowing clouds and wondered what Tritos was talking about. The hawk that she'd seen earlier flew back into her field of vision. Without even realizing it, she thought about how high it soared. Instantaneously she was lifted off the ground by unseen powers! She did not lift off in some tender fashion like a balloon or kite. Instead, she was propelled at an incredible speed, hurtling ever upward to the spot that she had thought about high above.

"Y

A

H

H

H!!!!!!!!!" was all that she could manage as the ground grew more and more distant. She fearfully wondered how high this device could possibly take her, and as a result, she unwittingly commanded it further upward. Just as she began to scream again, she realized that she had stopped and was now hovering perhaps a mile in the air. Tritos had apparently caught up to her and now had her in a firm bear hug from behind. He prevented any further ascent.

Merlena allowed herself to take a quick look down.

"No - do not think down." urged Tritos as he reached around from behind her to cover her eyes.

"How about I think about kicking your ass!" screamed Merlena. "Think up. Think up," she said while mimicking his voice. "What the hell Tritos! How about next time telling me how to stop before I go up!"

"My apologies. I did not realize that you would propel yourself so aggressively," said Tritos softly.

"Trust me Tritos, neither did I. Now give me a little more instruction on how to work this thing," replied Merlena. Tritos had removed his hand from over her eyes, but she continued to keep them squeezed shut.

"As I stated before, it responds to your mental commands. It is important that you clear your mind. Any indication of direction - up, down, left, right, here, there - will result in propulsion in that direction."

"So how do I hold still?"

"You are doing it now, keep your mind clear of directional commands."

Scared to open her eyes, Merlena flailed her arms to reach blindly about her. She had just now realized that Tritos had let go of her. She was hovering on her own in thin air, teetering back and forth as if balancing on some invisible plank. Still squeezing her eyes shut as tightly as possible, she screamed out, "Dammit Tritos, stop doing that! Why'd you let go of me!?"

"Self-reliance is sometimes the greatest tutor. Your anger at me is helping you to avoid inadvertent commands to the belt."

"That anger is gonna help me put my fist in your face if I can figure out how to get over there!"

"Let us practice just that. Look around you. Take in your surroundings, without actually thinking about getting to them.

Merlena cautiously opened her eyes and looked around. Clear, blue skies with an occasional fluffy, gray cloud surrounded her. It was such an odd perspective looking around (instead of up) at the sky. Before looking down, Merlena closed her eyes again and concentrated. It was going to be very difficult to look down without panicking or at least thinking about wanting to go back down. Though Merlena had never been afraid of heights, she had also never been floating in mid-air a mile above the ground.

OK, OK, KEEP COOL, thought Merlena to herself. *EVERYTHING IRIE, EVERYTHING IRIE, OK.* She looked down. Nothing happened.

No movement.

Good, keep it steady, keep it steady. Hover. Hover. Hover. Float, levitate, hang right here. While thinking these controlled thoughts, she took in the details of the Earth, far below her, as butterflies rampaged in her stomach. There was the Manor, laid out in all its grandeur. Beyond the acres of its property were other estates, some of equal stature. In the distance she could see the tiny specks of vehicles, in typical morning commute gridlock, on Interstates 270, 495, and 95. She wondered if any of the drivers were curious about what the tiny appearance of her airborne outline might be. The Potomac River cut across her view to the south, and beyond it lay congested northern Virginia. It was all a beautiful, yet intimidating view. This was an experience almost beyond description.

She thought about turning to face Tritos and immediately the Belt obeyed. He was staring at her intently, trying to read her emotions.

"It's beautiful," Merlena beamed. The rising sun gracefully outlined her delicately floating figure.

"Before the arrival of the Harvesters, I often would levitate high above Earth just to admire God's incredible artistry."

"I had no idea that you believed in God."

"Our language uses a different name to refer to God, but I have no doubt that there is one same, true creator in which we both have faith."

Merlena and Tritos drifted slowly toward each other and were now holding hands. Merlena actually forgot that there was no ground supporting her feet. She didn't notice the flock of Canadian Geese flying in their V-formation *below* her. She wanted Tritos to crush her in his powerful arms and smother her with passionate kisses. Though she would never admit it to herself, somewhere in the back of her mind she wondered what making love to her handsome host would be like here among the clouds.

Was it love that was making her breathing so laborious?

"I'm panting," was all that she could say.

"It is a result of the thinner atmosphere," responded Tritos in romance-shattering fashion. **"Think about descending ....very slowly,"**

Together they drifted down and leisurely reached the ground, still holding hands.

Throughout the remainder of the morning, Merlena practiced controlled take-offs and landings under the close tutelage of Tritos. After only a few hours, she began to feel much more comfortable with this fantastic new method of movement. It had been extremely difficult for Merlena to completely control her thoughts so as to not inadvertently command the belt. She was, however, beginning to get the hang of it. At mid-afternoon they stopped only briefly for a meal - and to be very sure that Merlena had fully digested it before she would return aloft.

As they stepped outside once again, Merlena asked "Do the Harvesters have Belts like these?"

"Yes they do. It is through the use of Levitation Belts that they have managed to remain undiscovered in such a populated urban setting. They can travel over rooftops unnoticed from the ground below. They also completely avoid leaving any footprint in the snow by hovering slightly above ground level rather than touching down."

"Yeah, I guess a nine-foot tall Maal would leave behind a pretty noticeable footprint."

"Precisely."

"Too bad. I was hoping these belts would give us a big advantage, but I guess not if they'll be using them too."

"Actually, their use of Levitation Belts will enable us to find them."

"How?"

"The anti-gravity forces emitted by the belts create a unique energy signature. If we are within about ten miles of the emissions, we will be able to detect them with a portable device that we shall have. The same device will pinpoint the location of these emissions to within a few hundred feet."

"So basically if they're using the Belts, they'll be giving away their location. But what about us, can they track us when we use the Belts?"

"No."

"How can you be so sure?"

"I invented and created the tracking device just recently."

"Cool." Merlena was beginning to feel a little more confident about the task at hand.

For the remainder of the daylight, she practiced using her Belt. Soon she had mastered take-offs, hovering, landings, and upper-air flight. Not bad for a girl who never had the opportunity in her impoverished youth to even try a bicycle. But now it was time for more difficult lessons.

"Attempt to follow me," instructed Tritos.

He flew off rapidly across the field behind the manor. At no time did his height increase more than eight to ten inches above the ground. Merlena cleared her mind, then commanded the Belt into action. Her keen intellect told her not to attempt directional commands, but simply to concentrate on catching up to Tritos' distant figure and allow the Belt to take over. Sure enough, as long as she had Tritos in her sights, the Belt did the rest. The difficult task was maintaining her height. If she flew too low she risked skidding her feet into the nearby ground only inches below her. At this rate of speed, that would surely cause her to crash. Indeed, the pace was intense. Both Tritos and Merlena were soaring across the snowy, open meadow heedless of any danger. Merlena knew from the outset of this chase that Tritos was headed toward the dense woods. Sure enough, upon crossing the field, he plunged in and was weaving himself around and throughout the thick, crowded trees and their many branches. He did so without slowing down even slightly.

Merlena was determined to match his pace. As the woods approached, her face became a forceful mask of concentration. Faster and faster she hurtled toward the upcoming line of trees. In the blink of an eye she was within them. She could see Tritos up ahead dodging a tree trunk here, a low hanging branch there. His reflexes were astonishing. As graceful as a sparrow and seemingly as fast as a rocket, he avoided all obstacles as he dashed through the forest.

For her part, Merlena had no time to admire his skill. She was maintaining her wild speed with every free thought directed toward catching her quarry. Few of her thoughts, however, were free. Never in her life had she needed to react so quickly. Near misses of branches tore like needles at her skin. Images of the hazards surrounding her began to blur due to the speed of their approach. She found it not only necessary to control the Belt, but to do so while contorting her body every imaginable way to avoid a tremendous high-speed crash.

Merlena's right arm hit hard against a tree at about fifty miles per hour. The impact sent her careening into a second tree to her left. The pain was immediate. She stopped and pulled a flask of Elsperium from a holster on her Belt and took a sip. Her now-dislocated left shoulder and fractured right clavicle healed instantly. She smiled grimly and pressed on. The collision left her far behind the rapidly escaping Tritos. Merlena redoubled her efforts to catch him.

An idea came to mind and painted a sly smile upon her face. She slowed her pace. Merlena reached into a pouch sewn into the thigh of her garment. She pulled out the Orem Sword handle and gripped it firmly. The blades immediately darted out to their full length. Like a machete through bamboo, Merlena sliced a path for herself through the countless, thick, overhead branches and burst upward and finally out above the tree line. With no obstacles in her path, she quickly gained ground on Tritos. Like some phenomenal gymnast, he continued to flip, jump, and duck his way past twigs, branches and trunks of trees while gliding just inches above the forest floor. As Merlena got closer and closer, he remained unaware that she had changed her tactic of pursuit.

As if surfing on the crest of some invisible tidal wave, she gained rapidly on her unsuspecting target below. Sword in hand, like some mythical Valkyrie, Merlena flew through the sky at tremendous speed. She looked down through the leafless forest branches at Tritos' fleeing form and prepared to dive headlong at him at just the right moment. Faster she flew and still faster. Her control of the Belt had become instinctual. No longer did she need to think about directing it. She simply allowed it to direct her. A few more seconds and she would be directly overhead.

Suddenly Merlena saw her opening. Down she dove. Her sword made glittering figure eight slices in front of her. Twigs and branches were obliterated from her pathway by the magnificent speed of her blade.

For his part, Tritos had drawn his Orem Sword at the first sound of a branch breaking overhead. His lightning-like reflexes would prevent Merlena's strike from being a surprise.

She halted her meteoric descent perfectly and now hovered inches off the ground in front of Tritos.

"Caught Ya!" she managed to exclaim between panting breaths. Though she had not done any running during this chase, the excitement and effort of controlling the Belt and wielding the sword had proven exhausting.

"The purpose of this exercise was for you to learn agility and quick reflexes on the Belt. You were to do this by avoiding the many obstacles in the forest at high speed. Your pursuit of me was to have remained within these woods, not in the sky above," Tritos stated dryly. **"You cheated."**

"But I won!" Merlena replied with a laugh. And with that she turned and glided happily back toward the manor.

Tritos was impressed. He had to admit to himself that she was right. He had wanted her to learn agility and reflexes on the Belt. Instead, she had broken the rules. But in doing so, she had proven her strategical strength and won this game. And winning, Tritos realized, would be all that would matter once they began their pursuit of the Harvesters.

For losing surely meant death.

Twelve

After returning from the Belt chase through the woods, Merlena convinced Tritos to allow her to show off her considerable cooking skills. Soon the delicious and powerfully spicy aroma of Jamaican jerk chicken wafted its way throughout the kitchen and surrounding rooms. It had been a very long time since Merlena had cooked a meal for a man. Merlena wondered what it was that made her want to do it so badly now. She pondered the feelings inside her that made her feel good doing something for her stoic, otherworldly companion. It was more than just gratitude that she felt toward him for saving her life during Cabbie's attack.

If only things were different, she thought to herself as she sliced up some vegetables. The carrots, onions, and potatoes on the chopping block in front of her were of peripheral interest as she wondered what a romantic relationship with Tritos might have been like. Then she almost giggled out loud, thinking of how awkward romance would be for the ultra-serious Tritos. *Do Maal even have such a thing as love?* she had to ask herself. Certainly, he'd shown no visible romantic interest in her. *Who knows, maybe he has a sweetheart back on Maalogg. Maybe he's just not interested.*

Merlena brought herself back to reality. These were ridiculously inappropriate thoughts. Soon she would be discussing a plan to apprehend the Harvesters. Merlena felt confident in her capabilities with both the Sword and Belt. Earlier, she had insisted to Tritos that they begin their hunt of the Harvesters tonight. They both knew that she would be better prepared with more training. But too many people were dying every night that they delayed.

Once all of the vegetables had been sliced, she put them in a pot of water on a low simmer. It would be about another forty minutes until dinner would be finished cooking. In the meantime, Merlena walked to the study to join Tritos.

The huge study was yet another of the many beautiful rooms throughout the manor. Stunning, massive, teak bookshelves stretched from floor to ceiling. Each was hand carved and inlaid within the perimeter walls of the room. They were packed with books of every imaginable genre. Volumes of history, anatomy, mathematics, chemistry, and science joined an equal amount of fictional stories of every conceivable variety. There must have been thousands. Each wall unit had a matching wooden ladder attached to rolling tracks. They were necessary to allow one to reach to the books along the top rows, which were as high as twelve feet from the floor.

Within the room were several brown, leather oversized chairs. Each was positioned next to a small, round, wooden table. The center of the room contained a large, rectangular, mission style, oak table. Four matching chairs were positioned around this table. Tritos sat at one of these chairs, poring over a map of greater Washington.

"Can I join you?" asked Merlena.

"Of course," replied Tritos.

"What are you doing?"

"I am studying the areas that have shown the most Belt emissions. They seem to be concentrated within about a five-mile radius. The Harvesters have found an area of comfort and will not move to another section unless they need to do so."

"Kind of like a fisherman who goes to his same lucky spot on the lake every time until he stops getting lucky."

"An accurate analogy."

She sat down in a chair across the table from him.

"So why that neighborhood?"

"They have chosen an area with victims that will not arouse suspicion once they go missing. The homeless, the indigent, illegal immigrants and even the criminal will not create any significant police investigation if they are never seen again."

"The Harvesters have made only two mistakes thus far. They did not properly dispose of the body of their first victim. It was discovered and now lies in the Southeast morgue. Their second mistake was to allow a witness to escape."

"You mean me."

"Yes."

Merlena shuddered as she thought back to that terrible night.

"So what is the plan? I mean once we track them down, then what?"

"We will make an attempt to apprehend them. If that fails, then they must be eliminated."

"Tritos....... I don't know if I can kill someone. I don't know if I'll have the courage. I don't know if I'm even capable."

"**Little less than an hour ago, you were insisting that we end the training. You stated that you were ready,**" said Tritos.

"I don't mean that I need more training. I'm just..... I don't know that I can bring myself to kill them..... it's a morality thing," responded Merlena.

"**Will it be more comforting to your morals to remain idle and allow multiple murders to continue each night?**"

"No, of course not. But-"

"**Just as in our training, allow your Maal instincts to take over in battle. You will not fail. You must not fail.**"

Merlena let out a long, exasperated sigh and got up from her seat. She forced herself to temporarily put her apprehensions aside. She paced along the edge of the room, randomly examining some of the literary titles. She changed the subject of the conversation to try to ease her mind.

"So how'd my father score all this?"

"**Pardon?**" asked Tritos perplexedly.

"This mansion, the manor, all of this luxury. How did he afford it? I mean even you - you didn't build it, but you must shell out a ton of money for its upkeep. You've had custom-prepared meals delivered daily. You must have landscapers, housekeepers, and more. How do you pay for it all? What do you do?"

"**Previously your father, and now I, manufacture the necessary currency.**"

"What do you mean?"

"**The money is printed off as necessary.**"

"Are you kidding me!?" exclaimed Merlena, with an incredulous smile on her face. "You're a counterfeiter? You print off fake money!?"

"**I assure you, the bills are quite real. They are exact duplicates of legitimate dollars of the United States. The paper, the dyes and inks, the plates, even the serial numbers are identical to those used by the real mint. Maal technology makes it simple**"

"But hello, that's illegal."

"**I can't very well announce my true presence and purpose to your government and request payment for my services.**"

"Maybe if you had, they wouldn't have hooked up with the harvesters."

"**Doubtful. As I told you previously, the Harvesters are most likely trading advanced weapons technology to this government, specifically the military. I cannot ethically match that deal.**"

"But you can ethically print off your own cash?"

"It is a small price to pay for my services."

"This mansion's no small price."

"That is true. Your father's love for your mother drove him to excess in the construction of this manor. I print off only that money which is necessary for its maintenance, and of course my living expenses."

"My father's love...... so Maal really can fall in love?"

"Of course."

"Have you ever been in love Tritos?"

"No," was his terse reply. He returned to studying the map laid out in front of him. For a brief moment, Merlena thought she saw a soft glow of purple color from Tritos' eyes reflected on the map. It faded out as quickly as it had appeared.

His body language suggested to Merlena that he wanted no more of this conversation. She returned to the kitchen to tend to her cooking. Her enthusiasm for dinner, however, had faded. Her mind now occupied itself with foreboding thoughts. Merlena had lost all joy in her culinary creation. Instead, she couldn't help but mentally compare this dinner to an inmate's final meal before execution.

Later she listened in silence as Tritos reviewed some cautionary rules for their upcoming patrol:

"Stay at my side at all times. Do not get separated."

"Keep in mind that you will be wearing the Levitation Belt. You must control your thoughts."

"If not enhanced, the Harvesters will appear as human as myself. When we arrive at the emissions area, trust no one, suspect everyone."

They would be leaving in a few hours. Merlena took some time to write what might very well be a last letter to her mother.

Thirteen

Mildred Bennett
Betheltown Post Office
Westmoreland Parish
Jamaica, West Indies

Mommy,

I know this letter must come as a surprise. It's been a long time since we've spoken in any way. I don't know how to begin other than to say that now I know the truth about my Father. I suspect that you've known all along. I'm sure at some point you witnessed his incredible strength or saw some emotion shine out through his eyes. Somehow I know that he must have been honest with you when he explained his abilities. I learned the truth myself just recently. I understand why you never tried to tell me the truth about him.

I mean I would never have believed you anyway.

You may not hear from me for a while and I need you to know some things before I go. I know I grew up angry and resentful because I had no father around when I was growing up. Alot of times I blamed you. Please forgive me. I know that must have hurt. Now that I know the truth, I feel embarrassed and ashamed at ever being angry with you. When I look back I can only appreciate how you worked night and day to keep us with food and clothes and a roof over our heads. Sure, times were tough, but we never starved, we never had to beg. You are an amazing woman, and I hope someday that I can be as good a mom as you are. I love you Mommy.

Say a prayer for me.

Lena

Fourteen

The temperature had warmed just enough to make everything a soggy mess. The falling snow had turned to a cold, frozen rain. It contributed to turn mountains of frozen snow into sloppy, wet hills of expanding, slushy ice. The streets and sidewalks began to resemble streams and brooks as they ran rampant with the combination of the heavy rains and newly melted snow. Many sewers were beginning to overflow from the liquid donations of the roadways.

The night's overhead rain clouds thoroughly blocked off any potential moonlight as well as any trace of stars. The darkness combined with the torrential rain to make visibility difficult at best. Washington area drivers were always in a hurry, even when weather conditions demanded otherwise. But tonight, driving was quite a challenge. More than one car lost control and skidded out of lane. As they drove along the Washington Beltway, Merlena peered out from her passenger-side of the front window. She could see little other than the taillights of the vehicle directly in front of them.

The rain pounded on the roof of the car mercilessly. The metallic din reminded Merlena of nights in Jamaica when the occasional tropical storm would batter the tin roof of their modest home. There was no fury on Earth like that of Mother Nature. Icy rivulets battled the defroster for control of the front windshield. The side windows had already surrendered.

The lone vehicle that had been driving ahead of them flashed its hazard lights and joined many others that had pulled over to the shoulder to wait out the severity of the storm. Through the torrent, Merlena could barely distinguish the reflected lane markers, but a glance over to Tritos assured her that he was having much less difficulty.

A random thought made her smile. "I can't believe you drive an old Hyundai," she said, lightly raising her voice to be heard above the pounding rain.

Tritos' brow wrinkled with puzzlement. **"What is it that you find so surprising about my ownership of an older Hyundai car?"** he asked. **"They are very economical vehicles. There has been no need for me to upgrade to a new vehicle. This one is in very good condition."**

"OK, sure. But I was expecting something futuristic. Or maybe really exotic, with cool gadgets, like a James Bond car or something."

"Obviously we could not operate inconspicuously in such a vehicle. It would stand out far too much."

"Yeah, well trust me, a car like this isn't gonna give anyone in Southeast D.C. a clue that an alien is inside. This is definitely a boring car." Merlena giggled again. "You're definitely a white Maal. I think a black Guardian would've bought himself a Porsche or a Benz or something. Definitely not a Hyundai."

"I do not understand why there remain such differences between the various races on Earth. Besides obvious cultural and language differences, there are social differences on this planet determined by skin color. This is the only world I know of where the color of one's skin very often determines the type of clothing, music, comedy, sport, career, and even type of mate chosen."

"Now you are informing me that even the type of car varies in popularity depending on the purchaser's skin color?"

"Uh, yeah. Hyundais have never been real big in the black community. I admit I saw some, as in very few, in Jamaica. But I've never seen any in my neighborhood here," replied Merlena. "Especially old Hyundais from the '90's like this one. Back then they were so boxy and boring. They weren't cool at all. Black people want more flair in their car."

"But why?"

"I don't know," she continued with a teasing laugh, "Hyundai sedans are just kinda conservative and dull... like white people."

"At least Earth white people anyway," giggled Merlena playfully.

"I don't understand why.." started Tritos.

"Why white people are so stiff?" interrupted Merlena.

"No," sighed an exasperated but amused Tritos. **"I don't understand why any differences in tastes or behavior here are determined by skin color. Why are the races here so different?"**

"Because races here were separated for so long. We developed differently."

"But transportation and economics have evolved enough to negate any distance on this planet. Any European can be in Africa tomorrow if he or she so chooses. Any African can likewise be in Europe. But even multiracial countries like this one still divide themselves into "black neighborhoods" or "white neighborhoods." It is rare to find a harmonious racially integrated community. Why?"

"I don't know Tritos. As much as white politicians talk about racial harmony, they still go home to their all-white neighborhoods. Black politicians are no better. Their first concern is for the black community that they represent. And why is the black or the white politician so desperate to please their own race of voters? Because they know that the other races won't vote for them anyway. It's just always been that way. It will be that way tomorrow. Barack Obama is a one in a million exception"

"Despite skin color differences, Maal feel a common bond toward each other. They are happy to assist each other. They act with a loyalty and affection toward each other simply because they share the same planet of birth. But Earthlings seem to seek out differences among themselves. They take pride in maintaining cultural, societal and even language differences. That baffles me."

"Wouldn't life on this planet be much easier and simpler if there were one universally spoken language?" Tritos continued. "Why continue to maintain borders and separate yourselves? Why can't the population of this planet view themselves as Earthlings instead of Israeli or Palestinian or Serb or Albanian or American or Iraqi?"

Tritos paused and shook his head. He wiped the gathering frost from the inside of his front windshield and squinted to get a better view of the road through the hazardous conditions. Then he continued. "Before the Harvesters began to sell their vile cocktails, Maal was nearly Utopian. Make no mistake, Harvesters are only a tiny portion of our population. But they cause more and more to become addicted daily. That is another reason why we must eradicate them, not only for the good of Earth, but for the benefit of Maal." Tritos once again cleared the windshield.

"Maybe there are so many differences between people on Earth because we don't realize that we're not alone in the universe," said Merlena. "Maybe we would all come together if we knew that Maal and other planets were out there." Merlena paused in thought. "Then again, maybe we're just always going to want to keep our differences. I gotta admit, I'm proud to be Jamaican. I'm proud to be black. I'm proud to be a woman. What's wrong with any of that? There must be some separations among the people on Maal. After all Tritos, you look totally white. My father looked totally black in his portrait."

"You are correct in your observation that I am of an all, as you said, white background. But that is very rare on Maal. Your father was racially mixed, as is most of the Maal population. It is very different there. Someday I would like to show you."

Merlena turned and stared at the cascading streams of quickly forming icicles running down her window. "I'd like that...... very much," she said softly. "It sounds like it was paradise before the adrenaline addiction began."

Just then a loud 'pinging' began to sound off. Tritos pulled up the sleeve of his coat and took his eyes off the road long enough to glance at a device on his wrist.

"What is that?" asked Merlena.

"The Belt emissions detector," replied Tritos impassively.

"Harvesters are near."

Just as they had anticipated, it appeared as though Harvester activity would remain within the same neighborhood that had already proven itself to be fertile hunting grounds. The continuing power of the storm had prevented Merlena from knowing precisely where she was. But as they exited the Beltway, she now knew that she was in familiar territory. A neighborhood park was off in the distance. On nice summer days, she had strolled down to its crowded basketball courts to watch pick-up games. Soon they would even pass by the hardware store where she had so recently been employed. A few miles away was her apartment. But that park, that job, and that apartment were from another lifetime.

After an all too brief intermission, the pinging from the Belt Emissions Detector began again. It competed with the force of the rain to dominate the noise in the car. "Even in this weather, Harvesters don't take a night off?" Merlena asked.

"**The hunger of their addiction is too great to resist,**" responded Tritos. "**Their personal need, combined with their greed for the profits that they will make from selling their plunder on Maalogg is irresistible.**"

Up ahead, a traffic signal turned to yellow, then red. Tritos brought their car to a stop. Merlena turned down the heater and wiped away some of the gathering condensation from her side window. She looked out onto what almost seemed like an abandoned appearance for this urban setting. The time of night, combined with the awful weather, had left the streets deserted. The only moving object to be seen was an empty Metro bus crossing through the intersection. Its great weight caused large, slushy waves to spout up from alongside its wheels as it hit a dip in the road.

"How do they control themselves from just using everything they harvest for their own addiction? How are they gonna have any left to bring back to Maalogg?"

"**Only a taste is required to cause enhancement, and its effect will last quite some time. As a result, the Harvesters can feed their addiction and still store the vast volume of their plunder for eventual sale on Maalogg.**"

"But how are they hoping to find any victims tonight? No one will be out there - this rain is totally miserable."

As if to support Merlena's observation, the rain began to pound down even harder. She scanned the side streets and alleys that they drove past as best she could for any potential prey for the Harvesters. "I don't see anyone walking around out there."

"**That is excellent,**" said Tritos.

"Why do you say that?"

"**It shall make it very easy for us to find the Harvesters.**"

"O.K. Why do you say that?"

"**The Harvesters will come to us.**"

"How do you know?"

"**Because we will be the only ones walking around out there.**" With that, Tritos parked the car at the curb and turned off the engine.

"You mean we're the bait?"

"**Precisely.**"

"Oh man, this is giving me a bad feeling."

Before they exited the car, Tritos went through a verbal checklist for final verification of Merlena's preparedness. Yes, she had her Orem Sword in her coat pocket. Yes, her Levitation Belt was on securely. Yes, she had her flask of Elsperium. Yes, she knew to stay near him at all times. Merlena silently thought to herself that he hadn't asked her if she was mentally prepared for this. But she knew that it was far too late for any trepidation now. Like it or not, she had to dive into this fearlessly.

Merlena opened the door and stepped out into the elements. She wore a full-length Slissen and Camac overcoat which included a large hood. The top and pants beneath the coat were of the same material. Her gloves were also made of Slissen and Camac. Fortunately, she and Tritos were of similar size, allowing this Maal armor of his to fit her well. He was outfitted identically. Earlier in the evening they had discussed the possibility of wearing the protective helmets and faceplates that Merlena had worn during Sword training. But it was decided that they restricted peripheral vision, hearing, and speech too much. That hazard would outweigh any benefit.

The outfit did an admirable job insulating Merlena from the cold. Still, the rain that poured down upon her seemed to touch every slight exposed area of her skin and spread an icy chill throughout her body. Merlena's nose and lips were already feeling drearily soaked and cold after only the few brief moments since she had exited the car.

She looked around and took in her surroundings. They stood in front of a small strip of stores. A laundromat, deli, video store, and barber shop all had their various metal cages across their storefronts to secure them in the overnight hours. Apartments, presumably, occupied the upper floors. All of the shops' lights were out except for the laundromat, whose red and green neon light flickered in the darkness. The street stretched out in either direction flanked closely by older, brick, low-income houses, apartments and storefronts. Not surprisingly, Merlena and Tritos remained the only signs of life to be seen at this hour and in this miserable weather.

"So what now?" Merlena asked. She tried to keep her head bowed as she spoke, in hopes that her voluminous hood would deflect most of the rain away from her face. "Do we just walk around and hope to get attacked by them?"

Precisely, replied Tritos.

"Great, can't wait," Merlena muttered sarcastically to herself.

Fifteen

"Christopher.... Chris can you hear me? It's me, Terry Loman." There was no way of knowing if the soft whisper reached the ears of the coroner's young assistant. This was the first time Terry had come to visit Chris at the hospital since he was brutally injured by the mysterious stranger at the morgue. There was no legitimate reason why Terry had stayed away. In truth, it was his fear that had kept him absent from the hospital. He knew that seeing Chris would bring back clear and vivid memories of that night. And though it had occurred less than one month ago, Terry had been successful in shutting out those memories as much as possible. He had shut them out just as he had shut out memories of the horrors of war in Vietnam and just as he had shut out memories of the thousands of faces of the corpses that he had seen in his career. Being able to shut out the thoughts of unpleasant sights was vital for a coroner.

Expressing sympathy and showing care was much more difficult for Terry. He liked young Chris Gavin a great deal. He had liked him since nearly the first day Chris showed up as Terry's assistant. Chris was fresh out of college and eager to succeed. Two years had passed since then and Terry's camaraderie with Chris had grown each day. But now that he had finally brought himself to Chris' bedside, he had no idea what to do or say. Terry never had a wife or a child or a sibling or even a cat or dog to love. This was a new experience. Terry was a father figure as well as a boss to Chris, but right now Terry could only stare down at the young man and weep.

The sight of the bandages covering the majority of the youth's face spoke volumes about the multiple surgeries that he had undergone since his nose and surrounding facial bones were shattered. The smashed cartilage from the bridge of his nose had been removed and replaced with a plastic support. It was his crushed cheekbones that were the greater concern. How well they healed would determine how permanently disfigured Chris would remain. As for now, the entire face was swollen to grotesquely comical proportions.

"Damn it Chris, why did you have to try to be so brave?" whispered Loman to the unconscious young man in front of him. Terry wiped away tears and sat down on a chair at the bedside. It was well past visiting hours, but Terry's city coroner credentials had gotten him admittance without a problem. The lights here in the room were only partially lit. The soft glow of several colors mildly floated in the air from the readouts of the various medical equipment in the room. No outside noise added to the soft whirs and gentle beeps of that equipment except the occasional footsteps of a nurse or technician passing by along the hallway.

Terry let out a long exhale and sat back in his chair. He thought to himself how peaceful the hospital seemed right now despite all of the suffering it must contain within its walls. He leaned back his head, closed his weary eyes and thought about the bizarre events surrounding the attack of his young apprentice. Seeing the suffering that Chris was enduring inspired Terry to redouble his efforts to catch his attacker. But to do that he needed to try to understand what had happened.

Terry closed his eyes and devoted thought to the many recent bizarre events: The body that started it all, drained of all blood. The stranger who came to examine the body and who so savagely retaliated after his attempted apprehension. The unidentifiable body. They all seemed to be linked by this mysterious Bennett woman. Her apartment had been combed thoroughly for evidence already by several outstanding detectives. But Terry had never been there personally. It was a long shot, but perhaps there was something, anything, that may have been missed. As skilled as those detectives may have been, they did not have Terry's experience or instincts.

Terry looked over at Chris once more. There was nothing more he could do for him here. There was no possibility that Chris would awaken from his anesthetic-induced sleep for a long time. Besides, Terry had wanted to sneak out before morning visiting hours began. He was uncomfortable enough already. If he had to interact with Chris' parents or family, it might be more than the hermitical Loman could bear. Terry got up and squeezed Chris' hand. He removed his still rain-drenched overcoat from a rack on the back of a closet door in the room and strode out. He was determined to find some clue of substance at the Bennett apartment first thing in the morning.

As he walked along the labyrinthine hallways of the hospital, Terry thought he saw a familiar figure round a corner up ahead and pass out of sight. Terry quickened his pace to catch up. As he got to the corner, he once again just managed to catch the man's back turn down another corner up ahead. Loman now elevated his speed to a light jog to catch up to the man. After turning the next corner, there was finally a long straightaway and from a view of only about thirty feet behind, Terry was able to clearly identify Chief Garnett.

"Psst, Chief." Terry whispered. Garnett hadn't heard and continued to walk away. "Chief," tried Terry a little louder as he struggled to catch up. Still no response. "Chief Garnett," said Terry at normal speaking volume.   In the silence of the surrounding halls, it virtually came across as a shout.   A nurse craned her neck out of a nearby doorway to shoot Terry a dirty look. Loman traded an apologetic smile and sheepish shrug of his shoulders to the nurse. She rolled her eyes and then resumed her duties in the room. Garnett, for his part, had stopped and turned. He looked as equally surprised to see Terry as Terry had been to see him.

"What are you doing here?" they said almost in unison. Garnett responded that he had been visiting Tom Pembleton, the guard whose forearm had been crushed, among other injuries, inflicted by the stranger who had attacked that night at the morgue. Terry updated the Chief on Chris' condition. Terry had rarely worked with Pembleton, and Garnett had probably never met Chris before this incident. Now Terry and the Chief both felt a little unspoken guilt for forgetting to visit the other injured party prior to leaving this evening.

"How is Tom?" asked Terry.

"Not good," responded the chief, "looks like he'll lose the arm. God I want the son of a bitch who did this. I want him so bad." Speaking of his injured man made Garnett's inner anger build to a crescendo. He nearly shouted his last sentence. Garnett punched the wall, further emphasizing his fury.

"I know I know," Terry said with true empathy. There was a brief silence that Loman quickly broke. "Listen, I'd like your permission to sweep the Bennett apartment again. I can't prove it yet, but I'm working on a theory that it is somehow related to the attack at the morgue. I know it's been swept at least twice already, but I'd like to do it myself."

"Of course, absolutely," granted Garnett.

"Will first thing in the morning be enough notice?" asked Loman.

"Why not right now?" demanded the Chief, still upset from the sight of his wounded officer.

"Uh, Chief its 2AM. Um, I'll need an escort in that neighborhood," said Loman.

"Are you here in your CC?" asked the Chief, referring to the City Coroner's official vehicle.

"Yes," said Terry.

"Are your kit bags inside?" asked Garnett.

"Sure," responded Loman.

"Then let's go, damn it. I'm your damn escort. Where are you parked?"

Loman led the way through the remainder of the mint green corridors until eventually they exited onto a pedestrian bridge leading to the parking garage. The rain had slowed little since they had entered the hospital, and now that they were exiting, both were glad for the roof over this foot bridge.

There was little conversation between these two aging veterans. Though they had worked for the D.C. police department many years, they had rarely worked side by side. Loman worked overnights, Garnett mainly days. They had little in common professionally and even less personally. But now they strode side by side in silent determination to find a lead to help them get closer to the attacker that they both so urgently sought.

Terry quickly found his way to the official city coroner's car. It was a white 1984 Chevrolet Caprice Classic with official city markings and a single rooftop flashing light. The nation's capital is not a wealthy city. Mismanagement, fraud and abuse have strained overburdened taxpayers' limits. The city education, sanitation, fire, and police departments must often compete over the meager funds available. After nearly a decade of pleading, the police department finally received a new fleet of vehicles in the late 90s. Unfortunately, the coroners' cars were not included in the upgrade. That was fine by Terry. It may have been twenty years old, but the Caprice got the job done. The old, reliable engine started just fine and began its ice-watery trek to Merlena Bennett's apartment.

As Terry drove along, he was thankful that the temperature had stayed above freezing and was forecasted to remain so. Any dip in temperature would have caused this deluge to freeze up. The higher temperatures would apparently help avert that disaster. He also felt thankful to be working so directly with the chief. Some may have found the task intimidating, but not Terry. Chief Garnett exuded confidence. It was an aura that Loman eagerly soaked up and it helped buoy his spirits.

Sixteen

Her body was aching.

Not so much from nearly an hour of random walking. Instead, it was caused by the anxiety of the anticipated attack. Her every muscle was tensed to react to the assault, not knowing at what moment or from what direction it might suddenly come. Tritos' damn detector was going off constantly. But as far as she was concerned, it was useless. It couldn't tell them exactly where the enemy was at, only that they were near. So Merlena could only wonder if the Harvesters were following her or merely traveling in the area. Each scrape of a tree branch against a gutter or rasp of litter blowing along the ground had made her jump back, poised to defend her very life.

Were they watching her? Did they sit somewhere on high, smiling grimly in hopes of soon feasting on her lifeblood? Surely they must be traveling in the air, making full use of their Belts. But there would be no telltale shadow cast by moonlight to warn her. The rain clouds above blocked any light that might have been cast by moon or stars. Again and again, the pinging of the detector. Finally, Merlena convinced Tritos of its uselessness. He agreed to shut it off.

So onward they walked. No particular direction, no master plan.

They were intentional targets.

Bait.

The very thought was emotionally draining for Merlena.

She had removed her hood some time ago. The heavy rain had made too much noise as it pummeled the hood. She needed every sense to be as unobstructed as possible. Now, with her hair drenched and the rain's icy tendrils finding their way into her outfit, a cold, hard weariness began to overtake her. Steps seemed to come slower. Tritos seemed to be getting farther ahead of her. The late hour, her drenched body, and seemingly endless walking made her thoughts drift. Scenes of her first encounter with these Harvesters repeated themselves in her imagination. Was her body trembling from the horror of these memories? Or had the cold, wet night now caused an uncontrollable shivering?

Merlena suddenly wrenched her neck to look skyward. Either her jagged nerves were playing tricks on her or she just sensed a large bulk pass overhead. Tritos was only about twenty feet ahead of her. He showed no reaction. Once again she questioned her mental fortitude.

Snapping herself out of her brief funk, Merlena jogged ahead to catch up to Tritos. She now kept her right hand in her pocket, ready to draw and extend her Orem sword at any instant. She looked over at Tritos. He, of course, showed no emotion. Neither his eyes or his facial expression betrayed whatever might be going on in his mind. Merlena could only wonder if he was scared or eager to confront the Harvesters.

There it was again. Not so much a sight or a sound to alert Merlena, but more of a *feeling* that something large had passed above and behind her. She whipped her body around to look, but saw nothing. Only the decaying, brick row-homes on either side of the street looked back at them. If they had been well-kept and in a nice neighborhood, the surrounding clusters of homes would have been described as "historic" due to their age. But no historian would want to lay claim to this rotting, graffitied neighborhood. It was a pitiful mix of empty, burned out crack houses bordering overburdened homes where sometimes as many as twenty members of an extended immigrant family lived together in a house containing no more than four rooms. These rowhomes were in what seemed like endless groups of five. An alley about eight feet wide separated each group. The alleys deserved as much scrutiny as the rooftops. The darkness of the alleys could hide an attacker as discreetly as any rooftop might. Merlena thought to herself how much easier this patrol would be if she could simply hover overhead to seek out a Harvester. But that would give away their abilities to the enemy and possibly cause the Harvesters to simply pack up and move on to another city. So Merlena and Tritos continued to trudge along the uneven, icy sidewalks through this hellious weather. Eyes and ears ever vigilant, each scanned the surroundings for any sign of activity.

A sudden scraping sound stopped them both in their tracks. Any sound in this empty, lifeless night would have stood out, but this was especially unsettling. There it was again - rising in volume above the hard rain, coarse and abrasive, high pitched and metallic. The gentle hairs on the back of Merlena's neck stood up and her stomach quivered. "What the hell was that?" was Merlena's whispered question to Tritos.

"It was the sound of Orem scraping against brick. I believe it came from the alleyway that we just passed," was Tritos' whispered reply.

Both Merlena and Tritos now turned and stared intently at the alley. Nothing could be seen from their vantage point. A thick curtain of darkness veiled whatever may lie within. They approached together. With each step, Merlena's heart beat faster. Inadvertently, she began to chew on her lower lip. She tried to control her quick, nervous breathing. A glance over to Tritos revealed nothing to her about what might be going on in his mind. He, however, could see her evident unease and took the lead in their cautious approach.

Merlena's heart was now racing. It beat twenty, perhaps twenty-five times between each step as she advanced toward the alley. Though silent now, there was no doubt that the eerie scraping sound had emanated from the alleyway - both Tritos and Merlena had heard it clearly. In front of her, Tritos had his unextended sword in hand. She removed her own from her pocket, and following his lead, was careful not to extend it. As they arrived within about ten feet of the entrance, both drew out the full length of their swords. A crash of metal sounded from within the darkness as a figure darted headlong at them!

Merlena braced for the worst - then let out a long held breath and laughed. A mangy cat was apparently the lone occupant of the alley. It directed an angry meow at the two who had disturbed its foraging in metal trashcans. Merlena drew back her sword and replaced it in her pocket. She wiped the rain clear from her eyes for a moment.

"C'mon Tritos," she said "they're not gonna be out tonight. We'll try again tomorrow."

"No. They are near. The device ..."

"The device is wrong," Merlena said, cutting him off with angry impatience. "Let's g-

She would never get a chance to finish the sentence. A blindingly fast mass slammed into her back with such extreme force that all breath was knocked from her lungs and she was left stunned. It took a full ten seconds for her to realize that she was now hurtling through the air in the arms of the very foe that she had been seeking. Grinning down at her with demonic satisfaction was a Harvester.

Merlena struggled to no avail. The creature's grip was suffocating in its power. However, he soon shifted that grip to rear Merlena back and hurl her down with full force from a height of about twenty feet in the air. She hit the ground so hard that she actually created a mini-crater in the slushy, half-frozen turf. Mud, slush, snow, and chunks of sod exploded into the air from the force of her crash. Woozy and dismayed, she struggled to her hands and knees.

Panic released itself and took over her thoughts.

Where am I? Where is Tritos? I'm going to die!!

No - get it together, you've got to defend yourself!

Get it together damn you - you're no coward!

She looked around. Swings, a seesaw, monkey bars, basketball courts. The Harvester had brought her to the center of the local park. The darkness and the distance from any street or house made it the perfect place for her death. But why hadn't he killed her yet?

Of course - he hadn't scared her enough thus far to produce maximum adrenaline. In fact, he would prefer to drain her while she was still alive.

Merlena forced herself to her feet and forced courage into her heart. She turned to face her assailant. From about thirty feet away she could see him in all his massive, deadly bulk. Powerful clouds of frosted breath shot out his nostrils with every exhale. He opened and closed his taloned fingers in eager anticipation of draining her blood. But the expression on his wicked face was one of bewilderment. Merlena smiled grimly, knowing that the creature must be baffled as to why the woman in front of him was not screaming or panicking.

Slowly, Merlena reached her hand toward her coat pocket to draw her weapon. She was prepared to slice this monster up or die trying. Despite the brevity of her training with the Orem sword, she truly believed that the inheritance of her father's genetics would leave her victorious in this battle. After all, hadn't she bested Tritos during training?

She reached into her pocket.

The sword was gone.

Seventeen

Tritos could only watch helplessly as Merlena was snatched away and carried off into the night. There was no chance for him to pursue; the remaining two Harvesters were diving down from the sky at a murderous pace straight for him. Only the inhuman speed of Tritos' reactions prevented their initial attack from succeeding. He hit the ground to duck down under the path of the first Harvester, then immediately jumped over the second. Instantaneously upon landing, he drew and extended his sword.

Here, in this unlikely interplanetary battlefield, Tritos stood. His muscles were tensed and poised, his eyes were blazing and his sword was held high aloft. What little light filtered in from outside the alley glinted off its razor edge. And now, for the first time since their recent arrival, two of the three Harvesters on Earth were suddenly aware that they were not the only Maal on this planet. The speed with which their intended quarry had avoided their attack, and especially his sword, served as a bold announcement that Earth's Guardian stood in front of them.

From the back of the alley, the Harvesters now drew their own swords. Still at the other end, Tritos stood his ground unwaveringly. An eerie silence took hold of the scene. Finally, after the momentary shock of seeing an unexpected Guardian had subsided, one of the Harvesters shouted to Tritos. The Maal language spoken in any manner would sound to an Earthling as harsh, rough, and perhaps even brutish. When shouted by an enhanced Harvester, it was truly fearsome.

Αρε ψου πρεπαρεδ το διε Γυαρδιαν? bellowed the creature in a deep, gravelly, bass voice.

Tritos made no response. He remained unmoved in his defensive stance.

δροπ ψουρ ωεαπον ανδ I ωιλλ κιλλ ψου θυιχκλψ. Ρεσιστ ανδ I ωιλλ τορτυρε ψου σλοωλψ! the Harvester tried again to elicit a response.

Tritos' silence seemed only to infuriate the creatures.

"Have you been here so long, that you have forgotten the proud Maal language!?" asked the same Harvester of Tritos, this time in English.

"Indeed I have been here a long time," Tritos finally responded.

"Your stay shall be much shorter. It ends tonight."

The alley was then bathed in blue light from the five combined eyes of the combatants. Tritos realized that one of his antagonists was the same creature that Merlena had impaled. That Harvester's intensity shone out through his lone remaining eyeball. This inspired Tritos with confidence, but it was imperative that he get out of the alley. The close quarters would make it easy for his adversaries to box him in, and that would result in certain death.

Tritos launched himself into the dark, stormy night. The Harvesters followed. High above the unsuspecting city, the battle began. As millions slept innocently below, their very future would be determined by gleaming sabers clashing in the inky, black sky. Without the benefit of starlight or moonlight, and well above the range of the streetlights far below, it was the uncanny, blue orbital glow of the Maal combatants themselves that cast a pale luminescence on their aerial combat.

The mid-air swordsmanship was dramatically amplified beyond that of any earth-bound display. Amazing levels of skill were exhibited as attacks, defenses, thrusts, and parries came not only from the horizontal plane, but also from above and below each warrior. Free from the constraints of gravity and like spinning gyroscopes, each fighter rotated at incredible speed as swords came together with violent crashes. Tritos found himself whirling into a near reckless blur as he devoted all of his considerable skill toward stopping the striking swords that seemed to come at him from all angles. This was his first true taste of battle. Tritos could lay claim to endless hours of Maal military training and computer simulations, but now for the first time, his mission and his life were at stake. The two Harvesters did not have the level of weapons training of Tritos, but in their enhanced state they were even more deadly.

Slowly, as the battle raged on, whatever brief confidence Tritos had enjoyed was withering away. Fatigue was beginning to creep into his muscles, and it brought desperation along with it. He now knew that he was overmatched. No amount of Guardian training back on Maal could have prepared him for combat against not one, but two Harvesters. As lightning-fast as his reflexes were, he could not keep up this pace much longer.

The enhancement of the Harvesters magnified not only their size and strength, but also their endurance. Their coordinated attack had kept Tritos on the defensive, and after nearly ten minutes of battle, he had yet to attempt his first offensive move. Already he had shown signs of vulnerability.

Now, not every sword stroke coming at him was being blocked. And though his Slissen and Camac suit did not allow the blades to slice through his flesh, the force of the Harvesters' strokes caused near disabling pain when they made contact with his body. He knew that if a sword slipped his guard and hit an elbow, knee, forearm, or shin, it would probably shatter the bone.

The light from Tritos' eyes slowly changed from blue to orange. This indicated an emotion that he hadn't felt since his arrival on Earth:

Fear.

At the sight of Tritos' orange, fear-induced emanation, the Harvesters paused in their attack and laughed with gusto.

Eighteen

Where the hell is my sword??? Merlena silently demanded of no one in particular. Panic ensued as she desperately dove down onto her hands and knees. She groped under the snow, slush and mud on the ground searching for the sword handle in vain.

From his short distance away, the massive Harvester flared his nostrils and inhaled deeply. His enhanced sense of smell allowed him to detect and savor the enticing scent of the sweet adrenaline pouring into Merlena's bloodstream. His mouth watered and lusted for a taste. He began to approach her. As he advanced, step by step, her terror heightened. The creature had no idea what she might possibly be looking for in the mire of the ground surrounding her. His only concern was to inspire maximum horror, and therefore more adrenaline, within this woman. To this aim he reared back his head, let out a terrible roar, and charged toward her.

Merlena abandoned her search for the sword and ran for her life. With more effort than her muscular thighs had ever produced, she sprinted through the park. Her shoes sank into and slipped in the wintry marsh that the park turf had become. Any thoughts of her Maal combat paraphernalia or brief training was forgotten in her fright. She weaved in and out of the rusted, metal playground equipment. She sprinted across the cracked blacktop of the basketball courts. But closer, ever closer, the creature pursued. Deep down, Merlena knew that he was toying with her, that he could catch her whenever he wanted, but she desperately ran on anyway.

Mere seconds later, however, she felt the crushing grip of the Harvester's hands on the back of her shoulders. He had finally caught up to her. Like a rag doll, she was lifted into the air then violently slammed into the ground. Though stunned and dazed, she courageously rose and tried to flee.

But once more she was grabbed from behind, and this time forced to stare into the hideous face of the monstrous Harvester who held her in his deadly grip. He bear-hugged her with one arm and slowly ran his clawed index finger across her face. Merlena's skin crawled from terror. She tried to scream, but could not. The Harvester tore off her hood and stroked her braided hair. He smiled a cruel, sadistic smile. Then, suddenly, he ripped a fistful of braids out of her scalp. Now Merlena's attempted scream was successful. Blood streamed out of the fresh wound in the side of her head. She screamed again in terror, fear, and pain.

The Harvester moistened his finger with Merlena's now freely flowing blood and brought it to his mouth.

He relished his gory treat and then spoke in a horrible mockery of English. "So good...... but not enough fear."

With incredible speed, the Harvester then launched himself skyward. In his brutally powerful arms he still clutched Merlena's helpless form.

This, the creature thought, would surely be the ultimate fear-inducing experience. High above the Earth, he dangled Merlena upside down by her ankle as he levitated leisurely above her. As she stared downward into peril, he uncoiled the needleworm from his backpack.

Floating high above the ground suddenly reminded Merlena of her own Levitation Belt. The thought hit her like a shot. Her training, her heritage, her mission, her destiny all re-emerged into her consciousness.

It can't end like this, It can't end like this! I won't let it!

With a primal battle cry, she twisted in the Harvester's grip and attempted to strike him. But as she contorted herself to reach up to him and attack, she had no time to dodge the tube that he drove deep into her neck. Right away she knew this to be the blood draining apparatus that she'd seen before. She could feel the needleworm crawl, no slither, in her flesh as it sought out her jugular vein. Still hanging upside down, Merlena tugged and pulled on the tube with all her might, but to no avail. Her strongest efforts could not tear the tube from her neck.

It can't end like this....

As she continued her fierce struggle to remove the tube, she could feel a small pinch within her neck. She knew that the needleworm had found its target. Blood trickled, then poured, then gushed into the clear tube on its way to the Harvester's backpack.

It can't end like this....

Her consciousness swam. Black patches appeared in her vision, and dizziness began to overwhelm her from the blood loss. She hung limply in his grasp and gazed down at the tiny lights of her city so far below.

It can't end like this....

She looked up at the murderer floating so casually above her. With one of his hands still holding her ankle, he used the other to reach behind his back to make some adjustments to his backpack. For the first time, Merlena noticed that he wore no Slissen and Camac armor. He obviously never expected to encounter a Guardian on Earth. The only Maal gear that she could see other than his Levitation Belt was his sword handle clipped to that belt.

His sword handle.....

His sword handle!

Thought was action for Merlena. With the last drop of energy in her body, she reached up and snatched the sword from the monster's holster. Before the shocked Harvester could react, Merlena had extended the sword. With one stroke she tore through the abominable creature's abdomen and sliced off his Levitation Belt. The Belt, along with some pulpy tubes of the beast's intestines fell toward the ground. Merlena concentrated all thought toward her own Belt and keeping herself from plunging to her death.

The Harvester screamed in pain and desperately clung to Merlena's ankle. It was taking a titanic effort for Merlena to keep both herself and the massive bulk of the Harvester afloat. Blood continued to rush out of Merlena's neck and into the tube. She knew she had only a few moments of consciousness remaining. With a savage sword stroke, she severed the creature's hand that was holding her ankle. The hand was hurled out into the night air, spasmodically gesticulating its fingers as it fell.

The Maal criminal's entrails continued to spill out. Its gory stump of an arm displayed a protruding, stark white, severed bone. Still it did not die. Though its Levitation Belt had long since been sliced off, the creature did not fall because the needleworm tube remained attached from Merlena's neck to the Harvester's collection backpack. Only Merlena's Belt and her force of will kept the two of them from plummeting to their deaths.

Every vertebra in her neck cracked and popped in protest against nearly five hundred pounds of Harvester weight forcing her out of the sky. Finally, Merlena drew up the sword once more and severed the tube. Her foe plunged earthward for nearly a full minute and finally crashed into the center of the park below. Tremors from the impact were felt in houses in a large radius surrounding the crash site. Sleepy residents stirred. Some awoke and briefly wondered what had caused the brief vibrations that had awakened them. But most quickly dismissed it and returned to their dreams.

Once severed, the needleworm was without its power source and was easily yanked off by Merlena. She used what little remained of her endurance to command the Belt to float her down to the nearest flat rooftop.

There she collapsed onto her back.

Wet, bloody, dying.

Anyone who could have seen her battered and brutalized body lying on the flat tar roof would surely have taken pity. But Merlena knew that she would have no rescuer to provide her with aid. She stared up through glassy, unseeing eyes into the starless sky. She no longer felt the frigid rain that now gently fell upon her. The rain mixed with the blood that leaked from her head, her neck, and countless other wounds. A pink puddle of the mixed fluids formed a perimeter around her prone form. Only her internal injuries surpassed the severity of her external wounds.

Nothing could revive her now. Nothing could save her from the eternal clutches of death. Nothing...except......prayer?

Even in her time of greatest need, she didn't ask for much. She prayed only for God to grant her enough strength to reach into her coat pocket. And for that pocket not to be empty.

"Please God, please let it be here," Merlena asked in a near lifeless voice. Her feeble fingers struggled to unbutton her coat pocket. Inside the pocket she found that which she anxiously sought. She pulled out her canteen of Elsperium.

"Thank you Jesus."

Indeed, it may have taken divine intervention to grant her the strength to twist off the lid and raise it to her lips. Still flat on her back, she poured the miracle Maal healing liquid into her open mouth and drained the entire contents. Immediately she could feel a wonderful warming and calming feeling overtaking her body. As the endless rain fell upon her, she closed her eyes, laid back upon this rooftop cradle, and allowed the elixir to work its magic. Without realizing it, she was soon asleep.

Nineteen

Dagger could only shake his head and mutter a curse. His hidden motion sensors in Merlena Bennett's apartment had signaled to him that someone had entered. But his hidden cameras in the apartment revealed that once again, it was only police investigators. *3AM, weird time for them to be in there*, he thought to himself. He looked closer into the monitor in his vehicle and zoomed in on one of the men. *Police chief? What the hell is it with this Bennett woman? Everyone who is anyone is trying to find her, but the press doesn't have a bit of interest in her disappearance.*

Dagger had basically lived in his SUV since his manhunt for this woman had begun. All equipment he needed to lead and direct his men and monitor the apartment was integrated into the vehicle. But despite thorough and aggressive investigation by his entire team, no new leads had developed. And so, never parked far from her apartment, he monitored everything. He had kept himself ready to respond instantly to any breakthrough, but none had been forthcoming. Now, the stress and strain of sleep-deprived days and nights were beginning to wear upon him. Dark circles were easily visible under his eyes, and an overall haggard, fatigued appearance had overtaken him. The stress of daily reports of fruitless results given to the Major was excruciating. The Major was not happy. Dagger had eliminated many, many people in the past who had made the Major unhappy. Now it was Dagger who was making the Major unhappy. Not good. Not good.

Random thoughts ran through Dagger's head. *What if I can't ever find her or her body? I have to give the Major something. There's gotta be hundreds of black chicks in this area alone that are a similar size and age. I could kill off one of them and say it was her. Have to use explosives, leave no identifying features. Yeah, hell I could do that tonight!*

No - no no no no. I don't know if the office has any of her DNA on file. If they do, they'll know a fake right away. Damn it!!! Where is this bitch!!!

Dagger punched the inner roof of his car again and again in his frustration.

Inside the Bennett apartment, Terry Loman crawled on his hands and knees looking through magnifying lenses clipped onto his glasses. He ran his deft, gloved fingers through the tan carpet looking for anything that may possibly have been overlooked by previous evidence collection teams.

It had been obvious from the start of this case that this apartment had been the scene of a vicious battle between at least two participants. One of those participants was now dead, another missing. A very competent D.C. forensics team had performed blood spatter analysis, fingerprinting, and fluid and hair collection. Bennett's computer files, emails, and internet searches had been examined. After exhaustive analyses of the scene, and all samples taken from it, nothing of substance had been learned. All fluids found had matched either the DNA of the John Doe corpse or Merlena Bennett (a sample of Bennett's DNA had been obtained from hair on a brush in her bathroom). It was, however, impossible for a woman of her size to have inflicted the injuries seen on the corpse. So tonight's search focused on finding proof, and hopefully the identity, of a third participant. No evidence of this mystery person had been found by the previous teams. But even the smallest item left behind could potentially lead to the biggest breakthrough in this case. So far though, Terry had found nothing.

Chief Garnett was just as dogged in his search. He had run a trained eye over every imaginable corner and crevice of the apartment. He had considered the contents of each dresser drawer and cabinet. Garnett even rummaged through the pockets of every pair of pants in the apartment. Items in the bathroom medicine cabinet, pantry, fridge and freezer didn't escape his scrutiny. But nothing had yet revealed itself as a clue.

Still, for both men, the hunt was only beginning. Each knew that a single dried-up drop of blood or saliva or even a single strand of hair could mean a big break in this confounding case. After a solid hour, nothing new had been found. Undeterred, both men carried on. The recent visits to their wounded comrades had served as more than enough inspiration to make this an all-nighter.

Twenty

From the cavernous depths of a deep slumber, she could vaguely hear the voice. It started as an indistinct, muffled sound. It was difficult to pick out, as if it were coming from a great distance or competing with white noise. She tried to shut it out, because as it grew stronger it pulled her away from the warm, soft nirvana in which she had been resting. There it was again-

Me.........na n..t m....ch ....ime get up

Because the voice insisted, she began to be drawn from the faraway gulfs of peaceful healing in which she had been residing. As her dream-state drifted closer to reality, she began to remember what had been happening. The surprise attack, the battle, the injuries, the rooftop.

......etup   ...erlena   we   mus..... go

The Elsperium in her body was adamant that she remain in this comatose state to better facilitate her healing. But her conscience and the voice calling to her would allow no further respite. Though seemingly held shut with leaden weights, Merlena was finally able to raise her eyelids. Sleepy, still groggy, Merlena took in her surroundings. She remained on the same rooftop, but her head was now cradled on Tritos' lap. He was scanning the horizon as he brushed back her hair and hadn't yet realized that she was awake.

At the sight of him, she snapped out of her haze. "Oh thank God you're here. Is it over then? Are they all dead?" she asked joyfully.

Tritos was at first startled by the sudden sound of her voice. Without compassion he looked down at her. **"Merlena we must go quickly,"** he said.

"I don't understand, why, what happened?" asked Merlena.

Tritos was silent for a few seconds, then snapped **"I could not defeat them! I ...."** he looked away in shame **"I retreated. It took all of my flying skills to escape. Come, we must go."**

"How did you find me?"

"You lost a massive amount of blood. I followed the scent of the adrenaline." He looked temptingly at the reddish-pink snow that surrounded them. **"Just as I found you, so may they. We must leave here with haste."**

"What are you talking about?" asked Merlena "Go where?"

"Anywhere! We must flee, we must go." He continued to anxiously scan the skies as he talked. **"They may find us at any moment."**

In the brief time that she had known him, Merlena had never seen Tritos like this. His confidence and steely demeanor was gone. He could almost be described as....... scared?

He began to scoop her up in his arms. Merlena tried to protest, but discovered to her horror that she was paralyzed below the waist. "Oh my God, I can't move my legs! I can't move my legs!" she shouted in panic.

"You have suffered severe injury to your spine. You finished all of your Elsperium and I have given you all that I had. It is keeping the area paralyzed while it fuses the severed nerves, blood vessels, and tissue."

"How much longer will it last?"

"I am unsure. It should not take much longer. Enough talk, we must go." Once again he attempted to lift her up, but again she resisted.

"No! Wait a minute dammit. Are you giving up? We can't just give up."

"We cannot win. Tonight, for the first time in my life, I faced off against real Harvesters. Previously, in training simulations, I had done it hundreds of times. Until tonight, I had thought that my weapon skills and courage would make me their equal in combat.   I was wrong. They dominated me as if I was a child. Their enhancement makes them invincible. I ran from them for my very life."

"But I -"

"Yes, I found the body of your combatant prior to finding you. Very clever slicing off his Levitation Belt in mid-air. Now, however, our advantage of surprise is gone. They now know us as Guardians. By now they have armored themselves. Soon they shall find you just as I did, by tracking the scent of this pool of blood reeking of adrenaline. If we are still here at that time, we shall die. We must return to the safety of the manor and await reinforcements."

"But you said that your reinforcements will take months to arrive."

"Correct."

"We can't do that. Damn you Tritos, hundreds will die by then. The Harvesters could move from city to city and we'd never find them."

"The only other alternative is to die tonight."

"No, we can do this. Put me down!"

After starting to carry her away, Tritos finally succumbed to Merlena's protestations. He set her down and gently propped her up against a brick chimney. Though he looked as if he wanted to say something, he kept silent and turned away from her. Merlena watched him as he peered into the night sky looking for any sign of their pursuers.

Due to her temporary paralysis, Merlena was helpless. This made her furious with herself. She tried in futility to rise to her feet. Though she could now feel a tingling in her toes, her legs were still completely numb and useless. She bowed her head in her hands. "I won't let you give up Tritos.

I won't let you give up."

"It seems that you will get your wish."

"Then you'll fight?"

"I now have no choice. Here they come."

Merlena looked in the direction that he pointed. She saw two figures in the distance, soaring through the sky in her direction.

At the blistering pace they were flying, it would be only moments before the Harvesters were upon them. It was too late to run or hide. Tritos drew and extended his sword. Merlena, for her part, was trying everything to get some life into her legs. She desperately squeezed them, slapped them, and finally hit them with no success. The pins-and-needles feeling that had started in her toes had inched its way across her feet to her ankles but she was still completely paralyzed below the waist.

Closer the Harvesters came. No longer specks in the distant night sky, their outline was now clear and distinct.

Merlena reached over and behind her to grab fingerholds between the bricks of the chimney. She tried frantically to pull herself to a standing position.

No luck.

Still closer the Harvesters came. Headfirst, arms at their sides, aerodynamic postures to maximize their speed. Their bloodthirsty hunger was now almost palpable.

Merlena flopped onto her belly. She tried to crawl to Tritos' side to fight in any way possible. It was no use, she was helpless. She looked across the rooftop at Tritos. She knew that he would meet the oncoming attack with heroic courage. But she also knew that he stood no chance against the creatures that rocketed toward him. Merlena's heart pounded wildly, her brain reeled, and terror filled her bloodstream with the adrenaline that the fast-approaching Harvesters so craved.

"**Merlena, I must tell you something before I die,**" said Tritos.

His back was still turned to her as he faced the oncoming threat.

The Harvesters would reach the rooftop momentarily.

"You're not gonna die," cried Merlena.

"**You know that I cannot defeat them in their enhanced state.**"

"Then enhance yourself."

The scent was unmistakable. Tritos turned to face Merlena. She had sliced open her wrist and the blood flowed freely.

"Take it baby, I'm scared as hell. Its gotta be full of adrenaline."

"1.... 1 cannot. You do not understand. 1..." A kaleidoscope of colors ran through his eyes. Lust, desperation, anger, guilt, shame and myriad other emotions blazed their Maal orbital color signatures.

"Take it, damn you! It's our only chance!"

Tritos leaped to her side of the roof in a single bound. He took up her bleeding limb to his mouth and drank deeply.

Twenty-One

Tritos' transformation was both immediate and horrifying. He stood up, arched his back, and howled into the darkness. Merlena looked up to see an expression somewhere between madness and exultation on his face. Physical changes were happening everywhere to his body at once. She could hear a sickening splintering sound as his bones stretched and expanded. His skin bubbled as it toughened and thickened. His voice became a deep, thick bass. Through it all, Merlena could not turn away. She could not tell whether Tritos' screams were from the pain of this terrible metamorphosis or from some sick pleasure brought on by the sudden influx of human adrenaline. The entire enhancement process took only seconds, but it had burned an indelible mark in Merlena's memory that she would never forget.

Standing in front of her now was no longer Tritos as she had known him. It was instead some terrible mockery of the man. Perhaps nine feet in height, with bulging muscles and taloned hands. But it was his face, the once striking, noble face that had most changed. Pointed teeth, a forked tongue, and a visage that would strike fear in the most stouthearted soul. It served as physical graffiti atop a once gracious facial mural.

The Harvesters had now landed at the far end of the roof. For the moment they checked their attack. They were completely confused at the sight here before them. What was happening? Had a new Harvester arrived on this planet? Was he friend or rival? They had thought that the woman lying prone beneath him was a Maal Guardian, but clearly she bled adrenaline. Could she possibly be human?

Tritos heard them land. He was torn. His body had already formed an addiction for the crimson delicacy coming from Merlena's wrist. He wasn't ready to stop draining her just yet. But, from somewhere deep inside his consciousness, his former self was screaming in his mind to get away from Merlena and attack the confused Harvesters behind him. He stared at Merlena's bloody wrist.

It was so tempting.

So warm,

So rich,

So good.

But with a moral strength more powerful than his body's new addiction, he forced his eyes away from her wound. When he was finally able to gaze into her beautiful eyes, he knew what had to be done.

Tritos turned, faced the Harvesters, and charged.

The battle was on.

The crazed behemoths did not fight like men. They fought with more ferocity than a pack of wild animals. Swords were useless in what had instantly become hand-to-hand combat bred of sheer rage. Teeth, claws, elbows, knees, and fists were constant, random weapons.

While they brawled, Merlena continued to struggle to rise. The Elsperium still active in her system had already mended her slit wrist, but had not yet finished the healing of her spine. As a result, she still could not stand. She remained an unwilling spectator to perhaps the most savage battle ever witnessed.

If some sliver of rationality remained in Tritos' brain, it was buried deep beneath hate, rage, and bloodlust. Like some rabid animal, he was driven by madness to maim and kill. He felt energy like never before, and with it he felt power. His enhancement convinced him that he was impervious to pain and fatigue. Bulging muscles rippled with each movement. Newly-grown talons on his fingers and toes felt good as they ripped into the flesh of his two foes. His self-sharpened teeth longed to tear Harvester skin asunder.

For a time, Tritos dominated the fight. He gloried in the pain that he was inflicting. But his opponents shared his same cursed gifts that came along with Maal enhancement, and gradually the tide of the combat turned in their favor. Soon their coordinated attack enabled one to get behind Tritos as he was engaged with the other. Tritos was grabbed around the throat from behind and held in a near helpless position. Try as he might, he could not break the vigorous grip of the Harvester. The other Harvester pummeled Tritos with fists, feet, knees, and elbows. Absorbing these blows as best he could, Tritos tried desperately to break the hold of the Harvester behind him to no avail. The onslaught of blows continued as he remained helplessly restrained. The power of each single strike that crunched into him would have been enough to kill a human or severely injure a Maal. In his enhanced state, Tritos continued to survive, but his body was slowly being destroyed. The Harvesters would not pick up their swords and grant Tritos a quick death. This slow, tortuous beating was more to their liking.

Through it all, Tritos pushed, pulled, and strained to move out from beneath the vise-like forearm wrapped around his throat. His ribs snapped from body blows. His sternum, nose, and clavicle had long since been broken. But despite it all, his inhuman determination had finally allowed him to move the arm of his captor from his throat to near his mouth. Tritos sank his enhanced, sharpened teeth into the thick forearm. They tore through the Harvester's skin and muscle. Tritos bit down even harder as the Harvester desperately tried to free his arm. But Tritos' jaw was locked, and despite the continued assault from the free Harvester, Tritos bit down even further into the flesh and soon found bone. With a sickening CRUNCH, he bit through the bone and in so doing severed the arm just below the elbow. The amputee flopped to the ground, howling in pain, the fresh wound spraying its brownish blood like some macabre fountain. Tritos pounced on his victim, this time using his teeth to tear out the creature's throat. Tritos rose slowly from his dead antagonist to face his lone remaining foe. The dead Harvester's blood and gore dripped from Tritos' mouth to mix with his own which flowed from countless wounds that he had already suffered.

Tritos stood little chance against the enemy that now charged him. Earth's Guardian now fought against a relatively fresh, uninjured opponent. The Harvester made quick work of Tritos. He battered the brave but exhausted Guardian to the ground. Still the evil creature did not let up. It stomped powerful smashing feet into Tritos' groin, abdomen, chest, throat and face. It continued until Tritos' efforts to curl into a fetal position for protection turned into a helpless, spasmodic wriggling. Finally, no movement at all came from the trampled Guardian's body.

Tritos was vanquished. His bravest efforts had only defeated one of the two remaining Harvesters. Now he lay exhausted, crushed, and devastated. He could only stare hazily upward with his remaining consciousness as his one-eyed assailant picked up an Orem sword to deal out Tritos' death. The murderous beast raised the broadsword high over his head to deliver the fatal gash.

The sword, however, would never strike.

Instead, it fell from his hand, clanged against the roof, and retracted. Protruding from the one-eyed Harvester's throat was the full length of Merlena's blade. The creature slumped dead to the ground and Tritos could see that Merlena had regained enough use of her legs to struggle up from behind the beast to kill it. As Merlena watched, it reverted back to its non-enhanced state. Death had finally released it from its addiction. Merlena's single swordstrike had saved Tritos' life, saved her own, and perhaps saved the world.

Merlena knelt beside Tritos' prone form and held his hand. She had held his hand with affection before. But now enhanced, it felt grotesquely huge and abrasively rough. She longed for the effects of the enhancement to diminish.

"Tritos baby, when will the adrenaline wear off?" she whispered. "We need to get back to the manor, get more Elsperium. You're hurt bad. I don't think I can carry you like this."

"Get......... away" Tritos croaked out through torn lips.

"Huh, what?" Merlena asked and pulled away her hand.

"Get away from me. GET AWAY!" Tritos screamed as he rose to one knee.

Merlena stood up and began to back away.

"You don't know what you're saying, it's not you talking." Merlena was very frightened. She backed off at a quicker pace as Tritos began to stagger toward her.

"Get away from me! I want you! I can't stop myself! I want to tear you open and drain you! Go now or I will kill you! Get away!"

Merlena now saw the full power of the addiction. Tritos was battling himself internally. His body was forcing itself toward Merlena to reap the gory prize coursing through her veins. But what was left of his rational mind was warning her to flee. She commanded the Belt to levitate herself out of his reach. As she suspected, he was too exhausted and injured to follow her. Tritos collapsed back to his knees and screamed out in rage and frustration. He slumped back down into the slush of the rooftop and stared up at her with malevolent eyes.

"Please baby, please don't do this," Merlena pleaded through her tears while hovering above. "You can fight this. You can do it."

"Please," she whispered, "*I love you.*"

Tritos now lay face down, collapsed from exhaustion. His chest heaved, still struggling for breath after his brutal battle.

Merlena gently floated back down to the roof. She was desperate enough to try anything to help Tritos reverse his enhancement. Perhaps a gentle touch or even.... a kiss could help his rational mind win over the battle for control of his body. She approached his enormous form. He appeared to have passed out from fatigue. She tiptoed closer, using extreme caution. Other than his labored breathing, no movement came from his body.

"It's gonna be alright honey," Merlena said softly and reassuringly. "I'm gonna take care of you. We can do it." She knelt beside him, laid a hand on his head and gently stroked his hair. "You're gonna be O.K."

AHHHHHHHHHHHH!!! With a murderous scream, Tritos suddenly turned over and lunged at Merlena with bloodthirsty intent.

As fast as the speed of thought, her Levitation Belt rocketed her up and away from him. The desperation move had cost Tritos all of his remaining energy and he collapsed back down to a supine position on the roof.

Now hovering safely above, Merlena choked back tears until she sobbed uncontrollably. She looked down with sadness and pity at the monster that she had created. There had to be a solution, some sort of way to save Tritos. She knew that she wouldn't find it floating here. Merlena doubted that she could locate the manor from this point. Returning to the car would be pointless because she had no keys to start it. Worst of all, the sun was just starting to rise and would soon make her visible in the air. She had to get out of here now.

Where can I go?

What can I do?

Merlena remembered that her apartment was only a few blocks from here. With deep sorrow, she left behind the terrifying creature that was once the man that she was just starting to love. She needed time to think. There had to be an answer. There had to be a cure. Merlena flew off toward her apartment.

Twenty-Two

Dagger had to watch for a full thirty seconds before he could believe his bleary, bloodshot eyes. Seemingly appearing out of nowhere was the object of his heretofore exhaustingly hopeless hunt. His dashboard monitor clearly revealed Merlena Bennett entering the front vestibule doors of her apartment building. Dagger pressed a button beside the monitor to change to a split screen - one view of the elevator, one view of the steps. How would she get up to the fourth floor? She chose the steps. Dagger went to full screen on the steps and zoomed in. It was her, it was definitely her!

He put on a broad smile and finally burst out with a laugh and shout of exultation. Then all joy was replaced by grave seriousness and he roared out a loud curse in anger. Dagger had forgotten about the police chief currently in her apartment. Curse after curse tore out of his mouth. Dagger could direct his verbal fury at no one but himself. Since he had left no member of his squad stationed at the apartment, he now had only moments to reach Bennett before she entered it and walked into, or got scared off by, the police. If the police got to her first, it would be so much more..... messy to gain custody of her. Dagger hated the idea of killing police. The immorality of it didn't bother him. It was just extremely difficult to kill them without attracting a lot of unwanted attention.

Dagger was only a few miles away. He floored the gas pedal, shifted into two-wheel drive, and pulled up hard on the emergency brake to intentionally fishtail his SUV into a U-turn. Surrounding cars slammed on their brakes and swerved out of the way to avoid a crash. Most drivers were miraculously successful in staying collision-free. Two slammed into the line of parked cars along each side of the road. They looked around for the maniac driver, but he was gone, ripping through the narrow streets at insane speeds toward the Bennett apartment.

Merlena looked neither left nor right as she plodded up the stairs. The creaks of the old wooden planks of the steps were silent to her. The odors of tobacco, marijuana, garbage, curry, fried fish, and mold that drifted from the surrounding apartments were scentless to her. The occasional shouts of domestic quarrels screamed out in languages from nearly every continent did not reach her ears. She was unaware of her surroundings. Her mind had remained on the rooftop with Tritos. All her thoughts and prayers were hard at work attempting to conjure up a cure for him.

The Elsperium had done an astonishing job healing her physical wounds. Mentally and emotionally, however, she remained quite dazed and exhausted. And so it was habit and familiarity alone that guided her down the rancid hallway of the fourth floor. It was not until well after she had turned the knob of her apartment door that she remembered that it should not have been unlocked. And it was not until she had stepped inside that she realized that there were two men with startled expressions on their faces staring back at her.

The silence lasted only a moment.

"Merlena Bennett?" asked a powerfully built, older policeman.

"Yes," answered Merlena after a brief hesitation. The man looked vaguely familiar to her.

"I'm Chief Garnett of the District Police. Why don't you shut the door, come in, and sit down." Garnett scrutinized Merlena as he spoke. She looked a little dazed, maybe fatigued or maybe high. Her clothing revealed that she had been out in the weather for an extensive portion of the night. In her hand was something that he couldn't recognize, maybe a flashlight. She didn't appear to be carrying any weapons, but he needed to be sure.

Merlena continued to stand in the doorway. She did not move. Garnett did not approach.

"You're not under arrest right now," continued Garnett, "but I need to make sure that you don't have anything on you that would make me nervous. Raise your arms for me, I'm gonna check you for weapons, then we can sit down and talk."

Merlena did not move. Her eyes scanned Garnett then gave a glance at the other man.

"That's Dr. Loman," said Garnett. "No one is going to hurt you. We just need to know what happened here and where you've been."

After a long, tense pause the Chief continued. "Ms. Bennett, I'm going to walk slowly over to you. Please raise your hands." Merlena did not react.

"We've met before, remember?" asked Garnett calmly and slowly. "You were in the hospital. You were telling me about monsters that attacked you. It's O.K., I can help you." The Chief was trying to play psychologist to reassure this mysterious woman, while at the same time trying to be firm so that she would follow his commands. Neither side of the approach was working for him. Merlena hadn't stepped in or retreated. As he approached, her body language told him that she was preparing to defend herself.

Garnett saw that Bennett was about to say something, but suddenly she turned to look out of the apartment and down the dimly lit hallway. Garnett and Loman craned their necks to look around Merlena in the same direction. The clamor of what sounded like a stampede of many booted feet was thundering up the steps. Closer and closer came the rolling din of creaking floorboards and trampling, stomping feet.

The source of the commotion became visible just seconds later. A team of six men in black military garb reached the top of the steps and advanced toward Merlena. Dagger, in the lead, supplied a name for himself as Sergeant Grant. He then proclaimed "I'm taking custody of this woman in the name of the Department of Defense."

"Like hell you are," retorted Garnett. "This woman is a witness in a police investigation. She'll be coming with me."

"Wrong," said Dagger icily. "She's a threat to national security and wanted by the Pentagon. That gives us the authority over you."

"I'm the Chief of Police of this city. I haven't been informed of anything of the sort. Until that's resolved, she'll be in my custody," said Garnett.

"There isn't time for this bureaucratic bullshit!" said Dagger. "Give me the girl!"

"Let's see some I.D. Sergeant!" demanded the Chief.

Dagger gritted his teeth and glared back at Garnett.

The commotion from the hallway could be heard quite clearly within the surrounding apartments. Some residents peered out of their doorways to get a look at the cause. They quickly slammed their doors shut and re-latched countless deadbolts at the bizarre sight of uniformed and plain-clothed police and military personnel arguing vociferously with guns closely at hand.

Merlena continued to stand in the doorway of her apartment, which had abruptly become the middle of a standoff. In the apartment stood Garnett and Loman. In the hall was the group claiming to be with the DOD. Both groups were insistent upon taking custody of her. Merlena didn't trust either set of men, especially this Sergeant Grant, and didn't intend to become anyone's property tonight. Even in the midst of it all, she could not stop thinking about Tritos. His wounds were severe. He had no Elsperium to aid his healing and could even now be near death from blood loss.

The loud bickering between Dagger and Garnett finally ended in a futile staredown. The small group of soldiers fronted by their leader now directed pointed glares of hate at the Chief, but Garnett refused to allow Merlena to be removed. A thick, palpable silence enveloped the entire building. No more words came from either of the feuding parties. Frightened residents, somehow aware of the danger, huddled in far corners of their apartments in fear of a stray bullet. Merlena stood poised, ready to strike, dodge or run without hesitation.

For seconds that seemed like hours no one moved. A droplet of sweat slowly made its way from Garnett's thinning, grey hair down to the side of his face. Dagger's anger showed clearly in every feature of his face. The malevolently furrowed lines of his brow, his sneering lips and bared teeth, and especially his menacing eyes silently screamed out intimidation. Still neither party backed away. The inadequate lighting of the hallway, caused by a bad fluorescent ballast, began to flicker wildly. Strange, mutated shadows of the military men randomly appeared upon and vanished from floor, ceiling and walls, like evil specters.

Finally, the least likely of the group to offer a friendly smile did so. "Listen Chief, maybe we should all take a deep breath," said Dagger. "Why don't we step inside the apartment and calm down. I'll show you my paperwork and get you in contact with the Pentagon so you can authenticate," said Dagger.

"That's all I'm asking," replied Garnett. Then, addressing Merlena, "Ms. Bennett, I'm afraid I'm going to have to insist that you join us."

Merlena did not like this one bit. The sudden diplomacy in the sergeant's voice did not sound genuine at all. But after quickly weighing her options, she concluded that resistance was futile against so many men with so many guns. She entered the apartment followed by Dagger and his crew. She didn't like the sound of the deadbolt latching into place after the door was quickly shut. As the Chief and the Sergeant whispered to each other, Garnett didn't seem to notice that the military team had formed themselves into a semicircle, blocking any possible exit.

Merlena noticed.

Out of her range of hearing, Garnett and the Sergeant continued to talk quietly, and now, much more calmly. Garnett even patted the other man on the shoulder and the two shared a hushed laugh. Merlena was as confused as she was nervous. *What the hell is going on? The Chief is locked in a room with six armed men he's never met and he's smiling? This is wrong, wrong, wrong! Why can't he see it?* Merlena saw that at least the coroner seemed to share her anxiety. He looked visibly uneasy and apprehensive. Merlena assumed that whatever golden BS the Sergeant was whispering to the Chief was effectively putting the older man at ease. But Garnett didn't notice that the smile that was formed by the Sergeant's smiling lips didn't extend to any other feature on the man's face. He didn't notice that the Sergeant's eyes especially had never lost the look of intense hatred and cruelty that they had displayed in the hallway just a few moments ago.

Merlena noticed.

Merlena also noticed that every one of the soldiers was staring at her. Their stares were easy for her to read. Of the five men, two were looking curiously at the unextended Orem sword handle that she'd been holding this entire time. Two others clearly held murderous thoughts in their minds as they looked threateningly upon her. The last man ran his lustful eyes along the contour of her breasts, down her abdomen to her thighs. Merlena didn't know why the hell these men wanted her, but if they really were from the government, she thought that they must know something of her Maal background or contacts. She also knew that they had no good intentions for her.

She turned her attention to their leader as he spoke up.

"Chief, let me start by apologizing for our sudden entrance and for being so demanding with you," said Dagger.

"Apology accepted," replied Garnett. "Now tell me what this is all about."

"Of course," said Dagger. "You asked earlier for some I.D." He reached into the vest pocket of his coat. "It's right here."

Dagger withdrew his hand, but no identification was in his grasp. Instead he held up a black pistol with an attached silencer. And before Garnett, Loman, or Merlena could react, Chief Roland Garnett slumped dead to the floor with two bullets in his brain.

"HOW'S THAT FOR I.D.!?" screamed a psychotically giddy Dagger. "NEED TO SEE SOME MORE!?" Dagger fired five more silenced shots into the corpse as his men laughed with glee. The high-pitched, almost squealing laughter of Dagger rose above all others. It was like some insane soprano in an operatic chorus of lunacy, performing an aria of madness.

Dagger now turned his attention to the coroner and shouted "ARE YOU READY FOR SOME I.D.?"

Loman instinctively put up his hands, clenched up his body and awaited the fatal shots.

Backed into a corner opposite Dagger, Merlena positioned herself in a defensive stance. She did not know how effective her Slissen and Camac suit would be against bullets, but she did not intend or expect to go anywhere alive with these men. She gripped her sword tightly and extended its full, lethal beauty.

"Whoa." Before he could fire at the coroner, Dagger's peripheral vision saw Merlena extend her Orem Sword. A weapons connoisseur, Dagger had to stop everything to admire the beautiful weapon in her hands.

Loman opened his eyes to see why he was still alive. He saw Dagger literally gaping at the splendor of Bennett's sword.

"Ms. Bennett," said Dagger, "that must be the most gorgeous weapon I've ever seen. After I slice off your head with it, it'll be the prize of my collection."

"Come get it," said Merlena with a snarl. She raised the blade aloft, ready to deal out death.

Dagger raised his gun and leveled it at Merlena.

"Coward!" accused Merlena.

"What did you say, you little black bitch?" asked Dagger.

"Guns," replied Merlena " are weapons for cowards. I'm standing ten feet away from you. You're afraid to come any closer? You want me dead? Come kill me! Why do it from so far away unless you're afraid?"

Dagger paused and licked his lips nervously. He knew that his men were watching eagerly for his response. He was very tempted to charge her, take away her sword and then strangle her slowly. In fact, if he hadn't gone without sleep from the moment he'd been assigned to find her, he would have had that little black throat in his crushing grip already. But the murder of the cop and the soon-to-be-dead coroner would take alot of careful cleanup to hide the bodies and any evidence of their deaths here. There was no time for delay. Once again he raised his gun.

He stared at her. *What is the deal with this unassuming woman in her crummy apartment with a fantastic sword? Why is she wanted by the police, the defense department, and who the hell knows who else? Why??*

"I've got to know something before you die," Dagger said. "Who are you? Why are you my assignment?"

"I'm Maal," was Merlena's simple reply.

"What the hell is Maal?" asked Dagger.

With a powerful, deafening explosion, Dagger's answer came crashing through the window and surrounding wall. Shards of glass, bits of plaster, and chunks of wood and brick flew everywhere from the force of the blast. Power in the apartment short-circuited. The lights surged, flickered, then popped, plunging the apartment into darkness. A thick cloud of dust filled the air. Merlena, Dr. Loman, and most of the military team had been knocked off their feet from the sheer force created by this sudden chaos. As they struggled to rise to their hands and knees, each looked in the direction of the explosion to see what could have possibly blasted through the outside of the building into the apartment.

As the dust began to settle, Dagger reached into a pack on his belt and withdrew a small but very powerful flashlight. Its beam toiled to cut through the clouds of dust hanging in the inky blackness. But on the other side of the room, Dagger could see something massive struggling to rise. Backlit from the streetlights, rising within the huge crater where the wall to the Bennett apartment had once been, was a shocking silhouette. The other members of Dagger's team shuddered involuntarily as they too looked upon the target of their leader's flashlight.

Tritos, in full enhancement, stood before them. He raised himself to his full, terrifying, nine-foot tall stature. He drew and extended his sword. Then he reared back his head and let out a blood-curdling battle cry.

Twenty-Three

Most of Dagger's team were able to shed their shock and confusion almost immediately. Their hard-core military training prevented their astonishment and fear of the creature before them from freezing them into inaction. Three men, including Dagger, pulled out automatic weapons and fired. Deafening chaos ensued as rounds flew everywhere seemingly from all directions.

Merlena dove to the floor just in time to hear shots whizz over her head.

From her belly, she watched as Tritos wailed in pain. His Slissen suit was preventing the bullets from penetrating, but apparently his Camac lining had little effect softening the impact of the shots. Tritos raised his arms to cover his face. His body convulsed from the force of so many rounds ripping into him at once, pummeling him over and over. Merlena could also see that the gruesome injuries that Tritos had suffered battling the Harvesters had not healed. She had no idea where or how he had summoned enough vitality to once again come to her aid. But it was very clear to her that he was dying. However, no amount of pain, agony, or injury could stop Tritos as he charged his nearest attacker. With a single stroke of his lethal blade, he sliced the soldier's gun in half. The severed barrel flew up into the air. Then, faster than thought, Tritos' left hand darted out and grabbed the man's face. Tritos tore the face, along with the front of the skull, from its head and threw it to the floor. Pulpy brain matter dribbled out the front of the mercenary's gaping cavity. Random nerve impulses caused the faceless corpse to remain standing and even take two steps before it crashed to the floor.

Even these brutal, battle hardened military men paused in abject fear from the sight of Tritos' savage attack on their comrade. As the enraged Maal charged another team member, everyone in the apartment scrambled. In the midst of the panic, not all bullets found their target. Missed shots ripped through the thin walls into adjacent apartments. Two team members, unaware that they had positioned themselves in a crossfire, shot at Tritos. They missed him but mortally wounded each other. Another squad member reached the door, but found the exit barred by numerous deadbolts. Ironically, it was this same man who had locked all of those deadbolts before Tritos' arrival to prevent Merlena Bennett's escape. As the man now fumbled to open them, he felt a strange cold feeling in his chest. He looked down with the seconds of life that remained in his body to see the blade of Tritos' sword protruding from his sternum.

The firestorm of bullets in the apartment now came from only two remaining men. Merlena jumped to her feet and attacked the nearest. He saw her in his peripheral vision just in time to swing his gun in her direction. A shot ripped into her upper left chest. The Slissen suit saved her life by blocking the bullet, but her pain was so intense that her entire left arm went numb. Still, with her right arm, she aimed a sword slash at the man's rifle hand and easily severed it off. Her return slash sliced through the man's kevlar vest and disemboweled him. A final, merciful chop cleaved his skull from the top of his head to his teeth.

Merlena wasn't cognizant of the brutality of her attack. Her mind and soul were consumed with battlelust. Once again, recently awakened Maal genetics had guided her body through combat. She turned to seek out another opponent. But this battleground of carnage that had once been her apartment was now silent and motionless. Merlena saw that only two figures remained standing. The beast that had once been Tritos was about eight feet away from her to the left. He stood with heaving chest on unsteady legs and looked ready to collapse from injuries and exhaustion. Dagger stood an equal distance to her right. He had backed himself into a corner. He had his pistol raised and waved it quickly back and forth at Tritos and Merlena.

The three figures formed a triangle of indecision.

For the first time in a very long time, Dagger was unsure of himself. He did not know what to do next. He had seen the monster's incredible speed. He knew that if he used even an instant to shoot Bennett, the monster would use that instant to attack. Yet as he looked more closely through the dim light at the creature, Dagger saw that it had ghastly wounds. Wherever its flesh was exposed - hands, neck, face, and head - that flesh was nearly torn from the bone. Some sort of syrupy sap-type of blood drained and dripped from its wounds onto the floor. Several joints looked dislocated. Its breathing came in labored, phlegm-obstructed efforts. Still, Dagger thought, it was a deadly threat.

Merlena was as concerned about an attack against herself coming from Tritos as she was from Dagger. After all, less than an hour ago Tritos had tried to tear her apart. Now he stood just a few steps away from her.

What's going through your head baby? she wanted to ask him. *Did you come here to save me or kill me?*

She, too, could see that he was dying. But she knew that if she turned her attention toward him, she would receive a bullet in the head from Dagger.

With bodies tensed and eyes darting wildly, Merlena and Dagger speed-shifted cautious glances toward each other and especially toward Tritos.

Though visually locked on each other, the audible effects of the aftermath of their shootout were now floating into the apartment. Merlena and Dagger could hear approaching sirens, and perhaps even helicopters, growing ever louder as they got closer. Screaming, panicked residents of the building were continuing to flood down steps and even fire escapes to pour out into the street below. Many had children in arm or in tow. A random gunshot was customary in this neighborhood, but the deafening roar of the war that had just occurred in the Bennett apartment was terrifying. A crowd of literally hundreds stood gaping up from the street at the massive cavity in the outer wall of their building. Though the sounds of combat had ceased, the crowd pointed and gesticulated wildly from the street below as they began to discern three figures, one impossibly massive, still in the destroyed apartment.

None of these sounds caused Dagger or Merlena to move. They remained fixated on each other and the wounded beast so near to them. Neither person attacked or retreated. But it was the sound of Tritos' great mass collapsing to the floor that Dagger and Merlena heard next. The wretched sound of his afflicted breathing had nearly stopped. Minimal movement came from the mighty chest. He was, by all appearances, moments from death. Merlena looked with pleading eyes at Dagger. She dropped her sword to the floor, raised her hands and begged "Let me help him, then you can do whatever you want to me."

"I've got all the help your pet monster needs right here," shouted Dagger.

He aimed his powerful pistol at Tritos' head and squeezed the trigger.

"NOOOO!!!" screamed Merlena.

Twenty-Four

It is truly astounding how few changes have been made to firearms in the last four hundred years. In fact, the basic method of firing a projectile has not changed at all. Pulling a trigger causes a hammer to strike a primer. This ignites gunpowder causing it to explode. The explosion blasts the projectile through a shaft at the target. Mankind has gone from colonial muskets and single-shot pistols of the 1700s to wild west revolvers of the 1800s to machine guns and automatic pistols of the 1900s to today with many updates but no real changes to the basic design.

In that same three-hundred-year period, most other technologies have changed dramatically. Transportation, for example, has advanced from horseback to space shuttles. Long distance communication has evolved from shouting loudly to cell phones. Cooking has developed from open fires to microwaves. Nearly any other technology can also be traced back to far more arcane and primitive roots, but not firearms.

Thousands of years ago, when early man first found the need to kill, he was limited to using his bare hands. He soon discovered that rocks and clubs made the job much easier. Knives, spears, and arrows soon followed.

Finally, one fateful day in ancient China, the firearm was born.

And so, the action that Dagger now took in squeezing the trigger of his gun was no different than any action he'd taken thousands of times earlier. It was also no different an action than gunmen hundreds of years earlier had taken. The trigger was squeezed, the hammer released and struck..... this time nothing.

Dagger hadn't realized that he'd emptied his clip in the earlier shooting. There was no bullet in his chamber. He reached toward his belt for ammo but Merlena had already pounced upon him. They rolled over and over toward the gaping hole in the wall. Residents of the building who had run for fear of their lives just minutes earlier, now stood looking up from the street outside. As Merlena and Dagger continued their vicious hand-to-hand combat at the precipice of the blasted-out wall, they now became more visible to the crowd in the street below. People pointed and shouted as they looked up four stories to see a man and woman now standing toe-to-toe trading blows. The commotion soon brought others out of their buildings, some with coats hurriedly drawn around sleeping clothes. Still others living across the street from the scene opened up their windows to peer into the massive hole revealing the battle.

Merlena matched Dagger blow for blow. Punches, kicks, elbows, and knees were traded with deadly intentions. Somewhere in Dagger's mind, he wondered how this woman could possibly stand up to and return his attack. He could not have known that Merlena's Maal genetics were guiding her every move.

Suddenly both combatants were bathed in blinding light. They jumped away from each other and shielded their eyes to look at the source of the light. A police helicopter now hovered just outside the ruined wall of the apartment. Its intense searchlight illuminated every detail of the destroyed apartment. From their vantage point, the chopper pilot and his crew saw the blood, the guns, and the corpses strewn throughout the apartment. Immediately, the crewmen drew their weapons while the pilot shouted through an external bullhorn for Dagger and Merlena to raise their hands. Merlena complied and was shocked to see Dagger do the same.

Debris was whipped about wildly among the crowd below from the powerful downdraft of the chopper blades. People struggled to hold on to their hats and caps. Even keeping one's balance was difficult. As police cruisers arrived, officers tried their best to push back the crowd, but their efforts were fruitless. Eventually a SWAT team forced their way through the crowd and began a cautious entry into the building.

Merlena did not want to make any sudden moves that would alarm the snipers on the chopper. Keeping her hands raised high and her body facing forward, Merlena looked away from the blinding searchlight of the helicopter and toward Dagger, who stood about ten feet to her right. He, too, had continued to keep his arms raised, but as she looked at his face she saw that he could barely hold back a grin. In fact, he looked as though he was about to break out in laughter. *What the hell do you think is so funny?*, she wondered. *These are the police and you just killed their Chief.* Merlena knew that something was very wrong. She knew that some scheme had been hatched within Dagger's psychopathic mind. She continued to look him over from head to toe but saw nothing suspicious. Nothing, that is, but that sadistic smile on his face.

For the first time, Merlena looked down from her precipice. The rising sun had just begun to illuminate the scene. The crowd of onlookers below had now swelled to hundreds. Several local news channels had set up their spots. With cameramen pointing their equipment upward, reporters babbled excitedly, barely taking a second to breathe while describing the scene.

Police cars continued to arrive from all directions. They flashed their lights, blared their sirens, and honked their horns to fight through the crowd. Another police chopper, off in the distance, was quickly approaching. Several news helicopters hovered far above the scene, filming the chaos. Lena looked down to see more black-uniformed SWAT members entering the building. She assumed that it would take them a long time to reach her apartment. They would be moving very cautiously to ensure that there were no hidden explosives or gunmen in their path.

Wait! Explosives! The thought hit Merlena like a shot. She looked again at Dagger, this time at his raised hands. Barely visible within the clenched fist of his right hand was a small metallic black ball. Dagger's thumb held down what looked to her like a detonator. *A grenade!* realized Merlena. *He's going to toss it in the chopper!*

"Hey!!" she yelled to the chopper. Dagger looked over at her.

But there would be no response from the helicopter crew. They had no chance of hearing her above their deafening motor and whirling blades.

"Hey!!!!" she screamed again, this time waving her arms as she tried in vain to warn them. Dagger blew her a kiss.

"DO NOT MOVE!" came the stern warning directed at Merlena from the chopper's bullhorn speaker.

"You don't understand!!! He has a grenade!!!!" screamed Merlena desperately. The crew didn't hear a word. She tried to point at his hand.

A bullet from the helicopter ripped into the floor at her feet.

"DO NOT MOVE AGAIN OR YOU WILL BE SHOT"

The crowd below collectively gasped and screamed.

Dagger was now laughing out loud. He was dragging this moment out, enjoying every second. Now the chopper crew's full attention was on Merlena. She shot a look of hatred at Dagger. In response he silently mouthed the word *KABOOM*.

Almost in slow motion, Merlena could see Dagger.....

slowly cock back his arm.....

release his thumb from the detonator.....

begin his throw.....

Merlena saw something like a streak of lightning smash into Dagger's back. The impact hurled Dagger and his grenade off of the ledge. He plummeted toward the ground for no more than a second before he and his grenade exploded into millions of pieces. Tiny droplets of blood and body parts rained down like a mist on the crowd directly below. The helicopter pitched and reeled from the blast, then sought higher altitude. The SWAT team making their way up the steps of the building froze in their tracks.

The force of the detonation threw Merlena back onto the floor of the apartment. Somewhat in shock and temporarily deafened, she struggled to cast aside her dazed confusion to try to understand what had forced Dagger off of the ledge. There, lying only a few feet from her, was her answer. Tritos was mortally wounded and too weak to physically move. Yet he had somehow summoned enough remaining lifeforce to command his Belt to levitate his broken and battered body and propel it into Dagger. It could be the last aid that Tritos would ever provide Merlena. As he lay before her among the debris of her apartment, Merlena watched as death released him from his fearsome, bestial, enhanced state. His face and body quickly changed back to the noble, regal Tritos that Merlena had come to love with all of her heart. The signatures of his horrible injuries remained, but Merlena hardly noticed them.

Merlena crawled over to him. Her gentle tears turned to uncontrollable cries of sorrow. She cradled his head in her lap and kissed his face and lips. Her tears streamed down her face and dropped down onto the man that she loved. She whispered a prayer for mercy upon her fallen hero. He needed Elsperium to live, but his canteen was empty. He had given all of his supply to her on the rooftop earlier.

Then, Merlena watched as slowly, ever so slowly, a soft, purple glow began to illuminate from beneath Tritos closed eyelids. Its luminescence grew until Tritos weakly opened his eyes and cast a lilac glow upon Merlena, who was on her knees, clinging to his broken body.

"Oh, thank you God," cried Merlena. "Your eyes, baby, they're purple. Does that mean you're healing?"

"Mer....lena," words were difficult for Tritos, but he bravely forced them out. "It is .... not.... heal...ing. Purple is love.

I will al....ways love you."

Tritos then closed his eyes. Merlena watched through her tears as the beautiful violet glow beneath his eyelids faded, then extinguished.

Twenty-Five

"No!" shouted Merlena through her tears. "I won't let you die on me."

She put a hand to his chest to feel for a heartbeat, but felt nothing. Upon further thought, she realized that she was unsure if his heart was even in that location. With great effort, she quieted her sobs and calmed her grief to listen closely for breathing.

Come on, come on. Breathe, damn you!

It was weak, feeble, and barely audible - but the breath she so desperately needed to hear from Tritos finally came.

The other sounds Merlena could hear (these much more clearly) were the shouts of the approaching SWAT team. They continued to advance within the building at a snail's pace, fearful of hidden explosives. But she knew that they would soon reach her floor and eventually her doorway. She also knew that if she didn't get Tritos back to the Manor's supply of Elsperium, his death was a certainty. What she didn't know was how to find the Manor from here. Nor did she know how she could transport Tritos there even if she did know the way.

Seconds, Lena, she thought to herself, *you've got seconds to figure all that out. You can't sit here crying. What are you going to do?*

Strangely enough, it was a muffled cough that brought about her revelation. There, no more than five feet away, attempting to hide under an overturned sofa, was the coroner. She could see the remaining tufts of curly hair on his balding scalp giving away his position. *What was his name?* she asked herself. *Lemon? Lyman?* Whatever it was, it hardly mattered to her.

An idea to save Tritos was forming quickly in her mind. She rummaged in the Guardian's pocket. *Damn! Empty!*

She tried another pocket, then a third. Finally she found them, the keys to the Hyundai.

"Doctor, I can see you trying to hide under the sofa," said Merlena. "I need you to come over here. I need your help."

"Not a chance," said Loman. He too could hear the SWAT team approaching. They would soon be here. He was determined to remain shielded under the overturned sofa until then.

"Doctor, please help!" insisted Merlena.

"I'm not moving," asserted Loman.

Merlena had no time or patience to negotiate. With a roar, she leaped up, extended her sword, and sliced the couch in two with one violent slash. The pieces fell to either side of Loman

The coroner looked with amazement and awe at the halved furniture to either side of him. "How can I help you?" he fearfully asked Merlena.

"Go over there, remove his Belt, and put it around your waist," said Merlena while pointing at Tritos' body.

"What are you talking about? Why do you want me to put on his Belt?" asked a confused Loman.

Merlena raised the tip of her sword to the coroner's throat. "I don't want to hurt you doctor," she said, "but I will if I have to. Now I don't have much time. I need you to do exactly as I say or this man will die. SO PUT ON THE DAMN BELT!!"

The SWAT team continued to inch closer.

Loman hurried to carry out her demand. To him, Bennett seemed to be mentally unbalanced. There was no telling what she might do with that deadly weapon in her hand. He knelt down, then unfastened the unusual buckle and yanked the Belt from Tritos' body. Loman then stood up and put the belt on himself. He involuntarily shivered as he felt a mild tingle run from the belt to his brain.

The SWAT team inched closer.

"Now quick, help me lift him," ordered Merlena.

"Miss, I think your friend is beyond any help," said Loman.

"Dammit, I know you're stalling for the SWAT team's arrival," accused Merlena. "Help me get him up or I swear I'll slice something off of you!"

There was no mistaking the authenticity of that threat. Loman gave her his complete cooperation. Together they bent down. Each grabbed one of Tritos' arms. They stood up and supported his body between themselves.

The SWAT team reached the fourth floor - Merlena's floor.

Merlena could hear the SWAT team approaching. It was impossible for such a large team to move silently with all of their heavy equipment. Terry Loman heard their approach also. He turned to Merlena and tried to reason with her. "Please miss, surely you realize you're surrounded. There's police in the hallway, and that's your only way out."

"We're not leaving through the hallway," said Merlena.

"How are you planning on getting out of here?" asked Loman.

Merlena did not immediately answer his question. Instead she instructed him to hold on tightly to Tritos. Loman did.

The SWAT team carefully approached the bullet-ridden remains of the doorway to the Bennett apartment.

"Look at me Doctor," said Merlena. "I want you to think up."

"I don't underst...." began Loman. But then, he could only drop his jaw in amazement as he and Merlena began to hover a few inches above the floor, with Tritos still firmly clutched between them.

The SWAT team now stood poised outside the Bennett doorway. Before bursting in, they paused to listen intently for any sounds of movement. They could hear a woman's voice speaking calmly to someone else.

"Doctor," she said, "you asked me how we were getting out of here. We're going to fly." Terry Loman's stunned silence continued. "Do you see that sunrise?" asked Merlena. Terry looked out the exploded wall of the apartment into the pinkish-orange sun on the horizon. "Think about getting to it......NOW!" commanded Merlena.

The SWAT team burst into the apartment just in time to see three figures fly out of the living room and into the sky at rocket speed.

At least twenty members of the media were assembled in various spots on the ground below, as well as in traffic choppers above the scene. All paused in their reporting as they saw the conjoined figures of Merlena, Tritos, and Terry Loman fly out of the apartment and soar into the distance. "I can't believe what I just saw," or an equivalent expression was said in unison by each reporter to television and radio audiences of thousands.

For the hundreds of residents that had spilled onto the streets to watch the ongoing drama, and for the throng of police surrounding the scene, there was only one word - astonishment.

It was all some surreal blur to Terry Loman. Colors, sounds, and scents whizzed into him, and past him, as he was propelled through the sky. Somehow, he thought he heard Merlena Bennett instruct him to concentrate on staying with her. He tried his best to do so, and magically, his body followed the command. As she accelerated, dove, rose, and turned in the sky, he did also. All the while, they continued to share the burden of Tritos' limp body. The speed and wonderment caused Terry to lose all perception of location. He had no idea where he was or where he was going.

After recovering from their initial shock, the pilots of the many police and media helicopters attempted to pursue the streaking trio. But Merlena and Terry Loman flew away from the scene at a speed too great to follow. It took only moments to outrun their pursuit.

Once safely away from the scene, Merlena set her group down onto the blacktop alley behind a small group of shops. It was still too early for any employees to have arrived. Only some small dumpsters and graffiti-tagged walls were present to greet them.

"Are you O.K. Doctor?" asked Merlena softly. She removed Loman's Belt to prevent any accidental takeoffs.

Loman was still in shock. Rampant adrenaline was causing him to shiver.

"Doctor, we have to hurry," said Merlena. "This man will die if we don't. I'll explain all of this to you as soon as I can, but you have to snap out of it.... please."

Her calm voice began to bring him back to reality.

"Let's set Tritos down," she said. They sat him up against a wall. "Doctor, there is an older Hyundai parked in front of this laundromat," began Merlena.

" A Hyundai?" asked Loman.

"Yes," replied Merlena. "Here are the keys. I need you to drive it around here."

As she put the keys into his hand, Terry finally shook off his awe. "Why do you want me to bring the car back here?" he asked.

"We need to load in Tritos," she replied. "I can't risk anyone seeing us out front. Please Doctor," she continued in a soft, pleading voice, "we need you."

Terry took the keys and started to walk around to the front.

"Thank you," said Merlena softly. Then her tone of voice turned deadly. "Don't drive away. If you double-cross me, I'll kill you."

Loman's slow walk turned to a run as he hurried to bring the Hyundai to Merlena.

Merlena heard the car start a few seconds later. After an anxious moment she was relieved to see it pull around behind the strip center and pull up to herself and Tritos. Terry helped Merlena lay Tritos across the back seat.

"Miss Bennett, now that you have your friend in the car, will you please let me go?" asked Loman.

"I'm sorry Doctor," said Merlena, "I can't do that."

"But why?" pleaded Loman. "I've done everything you've asked. You're not going to kill me, are you?"

"Believe it or not, Doctor, we're the good guys," responded Merlena. "I just need a little more of your help, and then I promise you'll go free. But no more time for talk. We've got to hurry if Tritos is going to live."

Loman looked at the devastating injuries on Tritos' body. He wasn't sure that the man was even still alive. "What more do you need me to do?" he asked.

"I need you to drive the car. I....well, I don't know how to drive," said Merlena quietly.

"What?!" asked an incredulous Terry Loman. "You mean to tell me that you can fly through the air with a belt, but you can't drive a car??"

"I never owned one, not many people did in my country.." began Merlena. "Look, just get in the damn car and start driving!"

Terry complied, and Merlena sat in the front passenger seat.

"Which way?" asked Loman.

"Get onto 495 going south. We're going to Potomac." answered Merlena. "Go fast, but don't get us pulled over."

Beyond that, Merlena didn't truly know exactly where to find the Manor. But she prayed that the portable GPS system plugged into the Hyundai had the address on file. As Terry drove on, she browsed back in the GPS and found a frequent Potomac starting point. *That has to be it,* she thought to herself. With a little trial and error, she figured out how to program it in as a destination. Merlena instructed Terry to follow the GPS' directions. She then looked into the back seat at her fallen warrior and silently mouthed another prayer. As if in answer, she saw the chest struggle, but succeed, in taking another breath.

Despite the fast speed at which Terry drove, the trip would still take nearly an hour. Merlena used the time to tell Loman everything. She relayed every vivid detail starting with her unforgettable blind date and ending with her arrival back at her apartment a short time ago. And though she thought for sure that he would think her to be insane, Merlena told all that she knew.

Occasionally Terry would interrupt to ask a question, but for the most part he listened silently. As crazy as stories of aliens and Harvesters and Guardians may have seemed weeks ago, they now seemed all too real. Merlena's information provided answers for every question that he'd had. He now understood the body drained of its blood, and the body of the cabbie that had lain on his autopsy table. He understood the flying belt, and the amazing sword. He could even forgive Tritos for injuring his assistant and guard. He even felt compassion for the dying Guardian for risking his life to safeguard the people of Earth. Loman no longer drove Merlena under duress. He now drove with purpose - to try to save Tritos' life.

Tritos never regained consciousness throughout the drive. His battered body continued to struggle for every breath. Occasionally, his body would involuntarily spasm, and at one point he convulsed briefly. Now that she felt that she could trust Loman, Merlena climbed into the back seat to try to comfort Tritos. There was little that she could do except to hold his hand, brush back his hair, and pray for him.

Tritos' breathing began to change. Its raspy sound began to get noticeably louder. A heavy phlegm-obstructed breath was followed by coughing, then a gurgling sound, and then vomiting of blood. Merlena quickly rolled him onto his side so that he would not choke on his own vomit.

Terry Loman recognized the symptoms. "He's hemorrhaging into his lungs," said the coroner, "if he has lungs. I don't think we have much time."

"Then we can't worry about getting pulled over," said Merlena. "Do what ever you have to do to get him home!"

Loman floored the accelerator. He wove through the crowded traffic, using the shoulder several times to pass vehicles. Seeing that his exit was coming up in four miles, he increased his speed even more and reached the exit in less than two minutes. Even the GPS could barely keep up.

Soon enough, he found himself off the beltway, and eventually on the streets of Potomac.

It wouldn't be far now.

Large estate houses with tree-lined driveways and massive yards passed by as blurs from the speed at which the Hyundai was driving. Terry listened carefully to the GPS as it guided him through several turns. He slapped the steering wheel in anger as he was forced to slow down because of the many twists and curves that they now encountered on the road.

DESTINATION 50 FEET AHEAD ON THE RIGHT, alerted the GPS. Terry could see the driveway entrance ahead.

"That's it!" shouted Merlena as she pointed to the same driveway.

Terry didn't slow down. He roared the car up the full quarter-mile length of the driveway at full speed until he had to slam on the brakes to stop just outside the front door.

Tritos had stopped breathing.

"I know CPR," said Loman "I can help."

"No!" shouted Merlena. "No time! Help me carry him in!"

Terry had no ideas as to what possible medical equipment could be inside that could save Tritos' life. But he carried Tritos' shoulders while Merlena carried Tritos' legs and they ran with his body to the front door. Terry balanced Tritos with one arm while he fumbled for the keys. There were many keys besides the Hyundai key on the ring. On the second or third try, he finally found the correct key for the front door.

Tritos' skin was turning gray.

Merlena led the way as she led Loman to the basement. There, they laid Tritos on the floor. Merlena ran to a cabinet and returned with a flask of Elsperium. She hadn't yet explained this miracle liquid to Loman, and as a result, he had no idea what she was doing. He stood back out of the way.

Merlena tore off the lid and poured the burgundy fluid on Tritos' face, then propped up his head on her lap and slowly drained the bottle into Tritos' mouth.

Nothing happened.

She ran off for more of the liquid. This time when she returned, she poured the Elsperium into the opened wounds that seemed everywhere on Tritos' body.

Nothing happened.

Merlena started to turn for more, but then stopped and shook her head.

If two full bottles of Elsperium hadn't yet worked, she needed more than Elsperium.

She needed God.

Merlena knelt back down beside Tritos and held his hand. It felt wet and pulpy. Brownish blood leaked out from injuries that had torn off a great deal of skin from the hand. Many bones within it were broken, almost giving the hand a shapeless feeling. Merlena put her other hand on Tritos' forehead, which also bled freely from lacerated skin.

Then she began to pray.

She prayed with an energy and fervor that she had never before felt. Love had inspired her to a level of faith that even this devout Christian woman had never before reached. Sometimes audibly, sometimes silently, she repeatedly asked God to save Tritos' life. She continued until she had to suddenly pull her hands away from Tritos.

She had felt something crawling upon his skin.

The shock of that sensation had made her jump back. But now, as she looked closer, she realized that she hadn't felt anything crawling on his skin. Instead, it was the skin itself that she had felt moving. Bones, blood vessels, and muscle moved inadvertently as they lined up and healed their broken or torn tissue. Not unlike zippers zipping themselves shut, Tritos' skin was sealing itself at all of its lacerations at once.

Tritos' healing had begun!

Terry Loman rushed over to watch. He was amazed to see the miraculous healing powers of the Elsperium. He stood enthralled, almost spellbound, as the bloody, battered, and broken body that he had helped carry down here repaired itself at a furious pace, thanks to this wondrous liquid.

Merlena, too, watched the amazing healing. She had seen Elsperium work its magic before. But this time, she was sure, it was not Elsperium that was at work here. This time God had answered the prayers of one of his most faithful.

In only a few more minutes time, Tritos was completely healed. He slowly opened his eyes, confused by, then cognizant of his surroundings. As he sat up, he looked upon Merlena. No words were spoken. None needed to be said. His eyes emanated a beautiful lilac glow. Merlena's eyes cried tears of relief. In unison, they stood up and embraced. Tritos kissed her softly on the cheek. Merlena returned the kiss with plentiful, smothering kisses of her own. They became lost in each other, hugging tightly, kissing passionately.

For just a moment, Tritos' mouth lingered near Merlena's jugular vein. He could hear the blood within it calling to him, tempting him, teasing him. Merlena's adrenaline was still potent and plentiful. But then he brought his lips back to meet Merlena's. The lilac beaming from his eyes intermixed with the tears streaming from Merlena.

Tears of happiness.

Tears of joy.

Tears of love.

Epilogue

"That should do it," Terry Loman said softly to himself. The last drop in the bottle of Elsperium dripped into Chris' I.V. bag. Terry looked out the small window on the hospital room door into the hall to make sure that no one had seen him. Turning back to Chris, Terry could already see subtle signs of healing in his unconscious assistant's face. Terry smiled. By morning, he was sure that Chris would be completely healed. Just to be sure, for the first time in a long time, Terry said a little prayer.

Once finished, Terry snuck over to the room of Tom Pembleton, the guard with the crushed arm. Fortunately, Tom's scheduled amputation had not yet taken place.

Nor would it.

Terry had one more bottle of Elsperium to administer to him.

Author George Graham was born in rural Bucks County, Pennsylvania. His wandering spirit has led him to spend periods of his life in Philadelphia, New York, American Samoa, and Jamaica. He has now settled among the beautiful, rolling hills of Mount Airy, Maryland with his wife and two sons. Contact George Graham at HHarvest1@Verizon.net

Artist Patrick Stacy grew up in Germany and moved around often, being from a military family. He eventually landed in the frozen U.S. east coast for a couple of decades, got his degree at UMass (what seems like a long time ago), and wound up wandering out further west, settling (for the moment) in Colorado. Patrick began illustrating at a young age as many often do. His inspirations came from classical masters such as P.R. Rubens and Caravaggio, to the modern masters like Frazetta. In 1996, he became one of the L. Ron Hubbard's "Illustrators of the Future" award winners. See more of Patrick Stacy's mesmerizing art at http://www.portfolios.com/pstacyart

Reader feedback, comments,
and questions are appreciated.

Please send your emails to:

HHarvest1@Verizon.net

Like the Book?

You'll love the merchandise!

Go to:

www.colorfulstitches.net

for a full line of quality, embroidered hats
and shirts featuring the Human Harvest Logo!